PERFECT TEN

The Off-Season, 1

K.M. Neuhold

Copyright © 2022 K.M. Neuhold

All rights reserved

The characters and events portrayed in this book are fictitious. Any similarity to real persons, living or dead, is coincidental and not intended by the author.

No part of this book may be reproduced, or stored in a retrieval system, or transmitted in any form or by any means, electronic, mechanical, photocopying, recording, or otherwise, without express written permission of the publisher.

Cover Design by Natasha Snow designs
Cover Photography by Wander Aguiar Photography
Editing and Proofing by Abbie Nicole

CONTENTS

Title Page
Copyright
Blurb   1
Chapter 1   2
Chapter 2   11
Chapter 3   23
Chapter 4   30
Chapter 5   50
Chapter 6   71
Chapter 7   80
Chapter 8   92
Chapter 9   105
Chapter 10   116
Chapter 11   127
Chapter 12   138
Chapter 13   147
Chapter 14   159

Chapter 15	172
Chapter 16	185
Chapter 17	199
Chapter 18	211
Chapter 19	225
Chapter 20	245
Chapter 21	254
Chapter 22	270
Chapter 23	287
Chapter 24	297
Epilogue	304

BLURB

A cheeky virgin, a surprisingly romantic bartender, one house, and six months of nothing but fun...

I came to Palm Island two seasons ago, confused about my life and desperate for a change. The island drew me in, but I'm still not sure why.

Maybe it's time I cut my losses and go back home.

But when the breathtaking, flirtatious, tattooed bartender I've been crushing on for ages offers to let me room with him this off-season, there's no way I'm leaving now.

I can't believe I've lived here this long without truly appreciating everything the island has to offer: the beauty of its untouched nature, how to catch a wave, the appeal of casual s... well, you know. But Ten seems determined to make sure I experience every last one, and then some.

Will this be the last off-season I spend here, or could this thing between Ten and I be perfect?

CHAPTER 1

BAMBI

I curse as the sticky red drink I'm carrying sloshes over my hand and splashes onto my white T-shirt. You'd think after two seasons, I'd have learned my lesson about white T-shirts at work. I give a tight smile to the man who throws me an apologetic look for bumping into me.

It only takes a fraction of a second for his expression to turn from contrite to heated, his eyes sweeping over my petite frame before landing back on my face. I try not to twitch under his appraising gaze, counting to five in my head so I don't come across as rude or dismissive before slipping past him to deliver the drinks. The counting trick is one I learned during the year I spent stripping. If a guy feels too dismissed, he won't tip as well. It's true when it comes to serving drinks *and* when taking off your clothes.

"Can I get you guys anything else?" I ask, setting the drinks down at a table where the men are too busy trading *fuck-me* looks with each other like it's their last night on Earth to even notice me. Which, I guess, isn't far off. Not that the world is ending, but it's certainly their last night on Palm Island—Handjob Island to the locals when we're feeling cheeky or immature. It's Labor Day, after all, the official last night of the tourist season before all of the vacationers head home and the ferry to and from the island cuts down to only one trip per week for six months, severely limiting the number of visitors until a new season comes around again.

I back away from the table, glancing down at my shirt again to assess the damage. There's a decent-size red stain, vaguely in the shape of a dick if you squint your eyes and tilt your head the right way. Or maybe I've just spent too much time here on Handjob Island, and now everything reminds me of a dick. Hazards of the job and all that.

I hustle back up to the bar, trying harder than I should have to not to blush, when the bartender and my coworker, Ten, hits me with his best smile. It's the same smile that keeps the tips rolling in and customers clamoring for a chance to crawl into his bed and get the *full* island experience, if you catch my drift.

Sex with tourists seems to be one of the main perks of working on the island…not that I would know.

"Huh, that kind of looks like a dick," Ten

says, and I snort, making a grab to catch the damp rag he tosses me but missing at the last second. It plops wetly onto the floor by my feet and Ten arches an eyebrow at me.

"You should know by now that I'm not athletic." I pick up the rag and shuffle over to one side so I'll be out of the way while he continues his frenetic pace of filling drinks and flirting with any and every man who looks in his direction.

"Which sport has soggy towel catching?" he teases, skirting around me to grab the bottle of tequila. His hand ghosts over my hip for an infinitesimal second, managing to brand itself there, just like every other nearly non-existent touch he's gifted me with in the last two years. Touches he likely doesn't remember the moment they end but stay with me all the same.

I give a weak laugh at his joke and try to swallow my heart down out of my throat as I hopelessly dab at the stain on my shirt, doing little more than making it wet. After another minute of uselessly fighting the setting spot, I give up, tossing the rag onto the counter and getting back to work. After all, if I don't help these men get drunk…someone else probably will.

Fine, I'm not exactly curing cancer over here, but the job is fun, at least for now.

I notice a couple of guys claiming a recently vacated table, so I head over, putting on a fresh smile as I approach.

"Hey, can I get you fellas anything?" I ask, dropping my elbows on the high-top table and leaning in so I'll be able to hear them over the din of the bar. The closest man, sporting a meticulously groomed beard and several tattoos on his arms, leans into my personal space. My body tenses on instinct, and I do my breathing trick again, forcing myself to relax and keep my smile in place.

"Are you on the menu, sweet thing?" he asks, his breath already reeking of booze. Either his friends have bionic hearing, or they know his game because they snicker and wolf whistle at us.

"Sorry, hot stuff. Closest thing I've got is a Dirty Virgin, which, in spite of its name, is heavy on the rum."

His friends laugh again, this time clearly ramping up to mock their friend over his rejection as soon as I walk away.

"Sounds good. We'll take a round," he agrees, shamelessly putting a hand on my ass.

I inch away as subtly as I can and then weave my way through the crowd, back to the bar. To my surprise, Ten is waiting when I get there, both hands braced on the bar top, glaring in the direction of the table I just came from.

"Was that guy bothering you?"

I frown and glance back over my shoulder at the table. Mr. Handsy has already turned his attention on someone else, who seems *much* more open to his advances, hanging on him and playing with his beard.

"No more than anyone else," I answer with a shrug.

"Hm," Ten hums, still glaring.

Oookay. "Can I get three Dirty Virgins?"

He finally tears his eyes off the table, pinning them back on me in all their dark intensity. The stern expression melts away, a flicker of a smile replacing it. "Coming right up, Bambi." He winks and gets to work on the drinks.

TEN

It's a little after three in the morning when I manage to corral the last drunken customer out of The Sand Bar. The last night of the tourist season is always a little strange. Another summer over, another year gone…six months on the horizon with sexual options narrowed down to the same few dozen locals or my hand. It's grim, I'm telling you. Not that the rest of the locals aren't fine as hell…

My gaze travels inadvertently to the sweet

and always suspiciously quiet—even after two years here—Bambi, who's freakishly focused on putting the chairs and stools up so he can sweep the floor.

Things around here are getting rather incestuous. We need some fresh meat or something. Otherwise, I might end up bedding down with Easy again this winter, and nobody wants that. Not me, not Easy, and certainly not Lux, who may be the only straight man on Handjob Island but is mighty possessive of his best friend all the same.

"Did you make up your mind about this off-season?" I ask over my shoulder while tossing the empty bottles I stacked on the bar into the recycling bin.

Bambi doesn't answer right away. It's only the sound of his shoes on the worn wood floor and the scratch of the broom that lets me know he hasn't slipped out and left me to close up the place on my own.

"I'm staying," he finally says, his voice quiet and a little raw sounding after a long night of shouting over the music and chatter. "For now."

"Good." I don't know if I cared one way or the other until the word left my lips, but now that I think about it, it is good. He mentioned a few weeks ago that he felt like the island wasn't finished with him, and you don't want to mess with a sign like that. She'll let you know when she's ready to let go. Until then, sit back and enjoy the ride.

And despite working together at the bar for the past two seasons, I barely know Bambi. Maybe this off-season will be the perfect opportunity to change that. The possibility of a new friend, six months of nothing but hiking, surfing, and parties, and another great year in the books. All in all, life is good.

"Still not sure where I'm going to live," Bambi tacks on, a hint of worry edging its way into his voice as he carries a full dustpan to the garbage can behind the bar.

He brushes past me, and I take note of how interesting it is that he never seems to recoil from me the way I've seen him do with overly friendly—or downright handsy—customers. I wonder what that's about. He's a full-on mystery, and maybe it's the months of free time stretching out in front of me right now, but I'm finding myself curious to unravel him...

Not like that.

I eye him up and down curiously, my eyes lingering temporarily on his cute little ass. Okay, maybe like that...if he's into it.

"I've got a spare room." Apparently, I'm full

of surprises tonight because that was the last thing I expected to blurt out.

He eyes me warily, his big, blue, doe eyes slightly narrowed, a crinkle between his eyebrows.

"You're inviting me to live with you for the next six months?"

Am I? You know what, why the hell not?

"You don't have anywhere else to go, and I have a spare room. It's perfect. Unless you want to take your chances with Trick, but I hear his spare bedroom has a sex swing, which he uses regularly."

Bambi chuckles, leaning against the bar, bracing both hands behind him as he considers my idea.

"Thanks for the offer. I might just stay in my apartment and pay Nacho's half. I haven't decided yet."

"Cool." I pull out the cash register so I can get my count done, lock this baby in the safe, and get my ass home to crawl into bed. "If you change your mind, the offer stands."

"Thanks." He gives me a sweet smile that lingers on his lips for a few seconds before he pushes off the bar and grabs the broom again.

He whistles to himself as he continues to

sweep. It takes me a few seconds to catch onto the tune, but once I do, I chime in with the melody. Our upbeat, slightly off-tempo whistling echoes around the silent bar while we finish closing.

When we're finished, I lock up, and Bambi lingers for just a few seconds in front of the bar, looking up at the unlit sign with an air of wistfulness about him. The streets are mostly empty, only a few determined partiers still out soaking up every last second of the final night, no doubt planning to show up still drunk for the morning ferry ride home.

"Does the end of the season ever make you sad? Like everything is ending?" he asks.

I scoff. "No way. The end of the season is only the end for them." I jerk my head toward a pair of drunk guys clumsily groping each other against the outside wall of the restaurant next door. "The off-season is all ours."

"I never thought of it that way."

I wander toward my golf cart, pausing halfway on. "Want a ride home?"

"Nah, it's a nice night. I think I'll walk."

"Okay. Think about what I said. The room is yours if you want it."

CHAPTER 2

TEN

I wake up slowly, a familiar feeling of freedom settling over me as consciousness finds me and I remember the tourist season is officially over. A whole other lifetime ago, an existence like this was inconceivable. Working only half of the year and making enough to do nothing but fuck around in an island paradise for the remaining half, does it get any better than that?

I wince as I sit up, the ache in my shoulder an unending reminder of how close I came to checking out entirely too soon. A rollover car accident nearly killed or paralyzed me. Instead, it ended up giving me a new lease on life. After I was back on my feet, I turned in my resignation at the hospital I was working at and hopped on the first ferry out here.

I didn't know why at the time, other than that I'd come here on Spring Break a few years before and something about it called to me. Maybe it was the beautiful men in various states of undress at all times, or the party atmosphere that really spoke to me as a then twenty-nine-year-old, or maybe that it was the complete antithesis of my life before the accident.

I may have come here lost and desperate to remind myself I'm alive, but I stay because I truly love the island.

I stretch my arms over my head, letting the silky bamboo sheets I splurge on pool around my thighs, my cock half-hard and stuck to my thigh, the sweat on my skin a constant in the balmy weather.

I reach for my phone and smile, seeing missed texts in the group thread.

EASY: The ocean, he calls to me.

TRICK: He? Isn't it standard to use feminine pronouns when humanizing things?

EASY: The ocean is all man, baby, and I plan to get ALL up in him.

LUX: I don't care what pronoun we use. I just desperately need to catch some waves.

TEN: I am SO there.

TRICK: Turtle Fuck Cove in 15!

I send a thumbs-up and fling the covers off, swinging my legs over the side of the bed.

While I pull on a pair of board shorts and run my fingers through my short hair, I find myself whistling the same song Bambi and I whistled last night while we closed up.

It takes me far fewer than fifteen minutes to get to the cove, parking my golf cart on the side of the road and unfastening my surfboard from the roof. The guys are already waiting, all clearly fresh out of bed and eager to catch some waves.

The last regular ferry of the season is pulling out right about now, full of well-fucked, hungover men on their way back to their real lives. And with all of them gone, it's time *our* vacation starts.

Trick cards his fingers through his long hair, attempting to tame it in the wind before giving up and just letting it fly around his face. He has an easy smile, his board tucked under his arm.

Lux is in the process of wrestling on his wetsuit while Easy tries hard to act like he's *not* ogling his best friend's bare ass. To be fair, it's a bit hard *not* to look. It's a damn fine ass. I'm surprised the man managed to find a wetsuit that even comes close to fitting, considering his massive stature. He's well over six feet tall and built like a brick shithouse. Easy himself isn't small by any means, but next to Lux, he looks downright petite.

He finally manages to get the suit on, and the show sadly ends.

"All right," Easy says, clapping his hands together and whirling in my direction. "End of season, which means it's highlight reel time. Best hookups, go."

He and Lux pick up their boards and the four of us head for the water. The soft, dry sand, warm from the morning sun, sinks under our feet until we hit the tide line, where the sand is wet and packed down, peppered with shells and washed up starfish. A small crab scuttles by and a warm breeze carries the ocean spray in our direction, misting us gently.

"I got dicked down by a certified five-donut cock," I boast, and Trick scoffs.

"Pics, or it didn't happen." Easy gives voice to Trick's apparent skepticism.

I roll my eyes. "Right, next time, I'll tell the guy to hold up a second so I can run over to the Tasty Hole to grab a half dozen for measurement purposes."

"That's ridiculous," Easy says sagely. "You should keep them on hand at all times."

I snort a laugh. "I'm telling you, it was a fiver."

"The five-donut dick is a unicorn. It doesn't exist," Trick argues.

"You have to believe in something, man," Easy argues, and I nod in agreement as we all wade into the water.

"For my money, I'll take a two-donut dick any day," Trick says thoughtfully. "Dudes with massive dicks get too big of a head about it. They think they don't have to put in any other work, just show up with their dick and you'll fall on your knees and thank them for their trouble."

I make a musing noise. "I can see your point, but if I'm being honest, I absolutely *will* fall to my knees in thanks to a glorious cock."

"A-fucking-men," Easy agrees and then looks over at Lux. "Sorry, man, too much dick talk."

His massive legs hang on either side of his board as he dips his hands into the ocean and then runs them through his hair to slick it back, shrugging as a relaxed smile twists his lips. "If it bothered me, I wouldn't have followed you to Handjob Island."

"Well, the good news is, we have completed another season without some poor, misguided soul thinking Easy was actually in love with them and dropping their life to move here," Trick teases.

"You don't know that for sure. The last ferry is leaving right about now. Someone could be camped outside the Tasty Hole as we speak, just waiting for him," I point out.

Easy groans. "It happened *once*. Besides, I tell *everyone* I love them. It wasn't my fault."

The three of us laugh and then turn our attention to surfing for a while. There's no beating the exhilaration of the perfect wave. There's an almost indescribable beauty to the rhythm of it, the back and forth of the ocean as steady as breathing and just as necessary. It doesn't matter how many times I've done it. It still manages to make me feel renewed, like a rebirth I don't know I'm desperate for until it arrives.

Eventually, we're back to floating on our boards, soaking up the midday sun, exchanging more sexcapade stories, and giving each other shit for the obvious exaggerations.

"So, any headway with Boston?" I ask Trick, who visibly cringes.

"He hates me, my plan sucked, but now I'm fucking stuck seeing it through."

"Your plan really did suck," Lux says, Easy and I nodding emphatically.

"Then why the fuck didn't you guys tell me that?" He splashes water in our direction.

"Dude, we *all* told you," I remind him.

He groans. "Then you should have tried harder to make me listen. I'm totally fucked now. I have *no* shot with him."

"It's in Harold's hands now," Easy says with an air of inevitability.

Harold Tellinson was the original owner of the island. He built everything from the ground up with his own two hands and the help of his soul mate and partner. Everyone says he was a hopeless romantic. I'm not sure I buy into the idea that he still haunts the island, making love matches like some claim, but I believe in energy. He put so much of himself into this place that the romance lingers even though he's long gone.

My stomach growls, reminding me that I haven't eaten yet.

"Let's go grab some lunch," I suggest.

"Anything but donuts," Lux deadpans.

BAMBI

"I feel like I came with a lot more," my roommate, Nacho, says, looking at the two boxes containing all of his possessions aside from the duffle bag slung over his shoulder.

I look around our sparse apartment and then back at him, a pang of sadness hitting me. Am I making the right decision by staying? It would be easy enough to toss all of my things into the leftover boxes Nacho didn't use and get on the ferry with him.

I haven't made any friends here outside of him. What am I going to do once he's gone?

"Hey," he says, bumping his knuckles playfully against my chin. "You're not done here. If you were, you'd know it."

I tug my bottom lip between my teeth and nod. He's right. Even though there's a part of me desperate to leave, to go back to the familiar and pretend the last two years were a grief-induced fever dream made up to cope with the death of my father, there's an even bigger part that I know won't let me get on that boat.

"Yeah," I agree, bending down to pick up the top box. "Come on, we'd better get moving so you don't miss the ferry."

He nods, grabbing the other box.

We step outside, letting the door swing shut behind us, not bothering to stop and lock it. That's one nice thing about the island: no crime, no distrust or fear. It's a community, even if I don't particularly feel a part of it.

Tourists are hauling ass to the ferry as

well, some of them shuffling along reluctantly, others clearly still half-drunk or hungover, the normal excited din of the island dulled to a sad sort of chatter. People saying goodbye, some making promises to keep in touch with men they spent their vacation with, promises that are going to be broken the moment their feet touch ground on the mainland.

"You decide what you're going to do about the apartment yet?" Nacho asks as we join the exodus toward the dock.

"Not yet." A familiar tension twists in my gut, making my stomach ache. I hate making decisions. I hate not knowing the *right* thing to do even more. Maybe there isn't a *right thing* in this situation.

"You can afford it on your own," he points out.

"I know." I try not to sigh but fail miserably. "I just hate the idea of spending all the money I've managed to save over the last couple of years. When I do finally leave, I want to have a nest egg, you know?"

"I get it."

"But I have to give Devil an answer in the next few days," I lament.

"Okay, what are your options?"

I blow out a long breath, my arms aching

under the strain of carrying the box. I stop walking to readjust my grip and then catch up with Nacho. "Not a lot," I answer. "I can keep the apartment by myself. I can take Ten up on his offer to stay in his spare room…"

"Whoa, hold the fuck up." Nacho stops mid-stride, and I slam into him from behind, dropping the box, its contents spilling out over the road.

"Fuck, sorry." I kneel and start shoving things back inside as quick as possible so he won't miss the ferry.

"Dude, forget the stuff for a second. *Ten* invited you to stay with him?"

I shrug. "He was just being nice."

"Honey-baby, you have been crushing on that man since the day you set foot on the island. Do not walk. *Run* to him."

I scoff, feeling my face heat as I finish picking everything up and get the box closed again. "I have not been crushing on him."

He arches one eyebrow at me as I get back to my feet. "Fine, you 'haven't been crushing on him.'" His hands are full of his own box, but I can hear the air quotes from his tone alone. "My point stands. It sounds perfect. You need a place, he has a spare room, maybe you can suck each other off. It's a win-win-win."

"Nacho," I sputter, my face no doubt a bright crimson at this point.

We reach the dock and slow to a stop. "Listen, I love you just the way you are, but I think it would be good for you to branch out a bit now that I'm leaving. Make friends with some of the other guys, explore the island a bit. You're never going to figure out why you're here if you don't put in some effort."

I nod, my throat aching at the realization that this is happening. The closest friend I've had in my adult life is about to get on this boat and leave me behind. God knows when I'll see him again, if ever.

"Don't give me that look. This is *not* goodbye," he says, reading my mind. Nacho sets his box down, and I do the same. Then he opens his arms for a hug. "You better call me, and I want to hear all about the adventures you have between now and the start of the next season. I swear if I find out that you spend the next six months holed up all alone watching movies, I will *swim* back here to kick your precious little ass."

I snort against his shoulder and then nod. "I'll try," I promise.

Nacho kisses my cheek. "I'll miss you."

"I'll miss you too." I clear my throat and do my best not to let the tears burning my eyes fall.

"I can help you bring the boxes onto the ferry," I offer.

"Nah." He looks around, spotting the first man who looks sober. "Hey, stud, give me a hand?"

I wave as he boards the boat, and he shoots me a wink back since his hands are full.

Maybe he's right. But can I actually accept Ten's offer?

CHAPTER 3

BAMBI

I'm having second thoughts before I even reach the brightly painted teal front door of Ten's house. I hitch my heavy bag higher on my shoulder, realizing a little too late that maybe I should have actually *told* Ten I was going to take him up on his offer before telling my landlord, Devil, that I wouldn't be staying and packing all my stuff.

I stop on the front porch and scuff the toe of my shoe against the concrete in an attempt to clean off the smudge of dirt that doesn't really matter but is a fantastic procrastination technique while I work up the nerve to knock.

He offered me the room, even made a point of saying the offer stands. Worst case scenario, I'll just go back to Devil and tell him I'll be staying after all. It's not like the place will be rented out from under me in the meantime. Only a few dozen locals live here during the winter, and there's more than enough housing to accommodate us all.

I take a long breath and raise my hand to knock, but before I make contact, it flies open.

"Oh," the man on the other side says with amused surprise. He's no taller than I am, with brightly dyed hair—rainbow streaks this week—that's sticking up in all directions. Even my very virginal eyes recognize sex hair when I see it. As if the hair isn't enough, his lips are swollen and there's a dark hickey just above his Adam's apple, the smell of sweat and cum clinging to him like cologne.

He drags a hand through his hair to tame it, tugging the silver hoop that's pierced through his bottom lip between his teeth.

"Goose, hey, I...um..." I stumble over my words. We've met many times. On a small island like this, I'd have to actually *try* not to meet the other locals. Plus, Goose is the keeper of the good soap.

"Hey, Bambi," he says cheerfully. "Ten, you've got company," he calls over his shoulder, leaving the door open as he slips past me, bouncing down the few steps and sauntering away proudly, not giving one ounce of credence to the phrase *walk of shame*.

I clutch the strap on my bag more tightly. Yup, I was right the first time. This was a *huge* mistake. What am I going to do, spend the next six months watching all of the other locals use the revolving door on Ten's bedroom? Oh god, he'll realize in no time that my bedroom door is *very* stationary. I can't think of anything more humiliating than him finding out that I'm a virgin.

I turn, ready to hightail it out of here and pretend like Nacho never talked me into this stupid idea. Unfortunately, I don't make it that far.

"Bambi," Ten says my name happily as if he's *pleased* that I'm standing on his doorstep with all of my earthly possessions stuffed into a bag.

I cringe, swallowing down my heart, which lodged itself in my throat at the sound of his voice, and slowly turn to face him.

"Ten." I smile, trying my damndest not to fidget.

He's dressed in nothing but a pair of *very* low-slung track pants, clinging to his hips, the V of his lower abdomen fully on display, not to mention the barest peek of dark pubic hair. The tattoos that are always visible on his arms and neck in his regular T-shirts are now joined by a darkly inked chest, as well as a simple rose on the lower left side of his abs and script that I'm afraid to stare long enough at to actually read.

For several seconds it's impossible to do

anything but gawk at him. It's not the first time I've seen him shirtless, but I've had the same reaction each and every time.

His eyes land on my bag, and his smile widens, making my heart go wild. Is he *happy* I'm here?

"You're taking me up on the room?"

"If it's still available." I shove my hands into my pockets in an attempt to feel less awkward but end up feeling more so, pulling them back out quickly and folding my arms over my chest. "If not, it's cool. There are plenty of places I could stay or even keep the apartment I was sharing with Nacho." *Or, you know, fling myself into the ocean because this is so fucking awkward.*

Without my permission, my eyes drop to the soft bulge in the front of his pants. Even given my introversion, I haven't managed to escape the island gossip, and the word on the street is that Ten's cock is well worth seeing. Fuck, I need to stop looking at his dick.

I force my eyes back up to his face and find him smiling at me in amusement. "Sorry, I'm a bit underdressed. I wasn't expecting company."

"Oh, no, you're fine. I mean, *it's* fine. No big dick." I cringe. "*Deal*. I'm sure your dick is…"

"Fine?" he guesses, not bothering to hide the teasing in his tone as he smirks at me.

Someone, please kill me.

"I should go." I point over my shoulder, set on heading down to the dock and attempting to swim back to the mainland. If I die, I die. At least I won't have to live with this humiliation.

"Come on, Bambi." He grabs me by the arm, his voice laced with amusement as he tugs me into the house. "I'll show you your new room."

TEN

Here I thought that a hurried blowjob would be the highlight of my day, and then Bambi went and made it even better. It's been a few days since Nacho left, so I was starting to figure that he'd decided to just stay in the apartment by himself.

"It's not much, but there's a pretty decent view," I tell him as I push open the door to the second bedroom. Light spills in from the two large windows, a perfect view of the mountains visible through them.

"More than decent," he says, dropping his bag and wandering over to look out.

There's a stripped-down bed left by my roommate from a few years ago and an empty dresser. All in all, it's not bad.

"You have your own bathroom." I walk

over and open that door as well to show him.

"There's a bathtub," he groans.

Maybe it's because my dick is still fully in fuck mode, but the sound is downright filthy.

"Yeah, I spent a fortune to get a hot water heater over here, and Lux helped me set it up. I've never had any issues with it, so you should be able to enjoy a nice soak if that's your thing. It's not quite good enough to run two showers at once, but I'm sure we'll figure out a schedule that works for both of us."

I realize I'm rambling a bit, but Bambi is so quiet that it's making me nervous.

"Let me show you the rest of the house," I offer.

He follows me out of the room, and I point out my bedroom, kitchen, back porch, living room...

"Oh." He makes an excited sound when he sees the large wire cage in the corner of the living room.

"Those are my pet rats: Fred and Barney." I walk over to the cage and give a little whistle. One little pink nose peeks out of the hammock, twitching with the effort of determining whether I have a treat for him or if I'm just interrupting his nap. I pick up the bag of peanut butter dog biscuits and pull one out. At the sound of it snapping in half, both boys stick their heads out.

"They're so cute," he coos. "Are they friendly?"

"Very." I open the door, hand each of them a treat, and then scoop Barney out. He's all black and more than a little hefty from a bit too much spoiling. Fred ducks his head back into his hiding place to enjoy his treat in peace. I hold Barney out toward Bambi, who nervously cups his hands to make a place for him.

"Oh, he's kind of chunky."

"Full figured," I chide, and he chuckles.

"Yes, my apologies. You are a beautiful boy, aren't you?" he praises, figuring out how to hold him comfortably. Barney munches on his treat happily, not at all bothered by the new human in his life.

When he's finished, he scurries up Bambi's arm. Bambi giggles as the rat explores him, the sound drawing a smile to my face.

I think I'm going to like having Bambi live here.

CHAPTER 4

TEN

After the tour, I leave Bambi to settle in, wandering back to my room to get cleaned up and more presentable. I wrinkle my nose at the sex smell wafting off me as I strip out of my pants, tossing them into my dirty clothes pile before hopping into the shower.

I can't wipe the smile off my face as I grab for the brand-new bar of soap Goose dropped off for me. The man makes magic soap, I swear. It smells better than anything else I've ever smelled, and it always leaves my skin so smooth. There's a reason everyone on the island, including the resort hotel, keeps him busy making fresh batches to sell.

The two of us hooking up felt more like habit than anything. In fact, the more I think about it, that's what most of my sex life has been lately—checking boxes, doing what I've always done. Where's the excitement and passion I fell so in love with when I first moved to the island?

I huff a laugh at myself as I rinse the suds

off my body. Leave it to me to get all introspective about sex. Some things are meant to be enjoyed, not analyzed, right?

Once I'm dried off and dressed, I find myself heading back down the hall to Bambi's room. I should make sure he's settling in well, shouldn't I?

"Yeah?" he calls out when I knock.

I ease his door open and linger in the doorway, looking around at the room now that he's unpacked. He doesn't have much—the island life lends to being a bit spartan, so it's not surprising—but there are a few knick-knacks on the nightstand: a picture of him and a man who looks like he's probably Bambi's dad, a seashell, a shot glass from The Sand Bar.

He must notice my gaze lingering on it because he hurries to explain.

"I accidentally took it home one night. I was going to bring it back, but I figured Boston wouldn't miss just one glass, and it will be a nice memento of my time here when I eventually leave."

The reminder that he's not here for the long haul wipes the smile right off my face. It's likely this is the one and only off-season I'll have the chance to get to know him, to pull him out of his shell and show him a good time, so I can't waste a moment.

"Don't worry, I won't rat you out to Boston," I promise with a grin. "Actually, I wanted to see if you're planning on going to the beach tonight."

"The beach?" he asks.

"Yeah, there's a party down on the private beach. You know, bonfire, booze, probably some s'mores once Lyric is stoned enough to start making them for everyone."

"Oh, uh…"

There are parties nearly every night the first few weeks of the off-season, all the locals blowing off steam after a long, busy six months. They're typically open-invite. Just wander around the beaches until you find one and someone hands you a drink.

"It's going to be a good time," I tempt when he doesn't respond right away.

He tugs his bottom lip between his teeth, chewing it for a few seconds while seeming to consider the invite. "Yeah, I'll probably go."

I smile even wider. "Awesome. We can walk down together later."

"Great." Bambi grins back finally, still looking a little nervous but cautiously excited.

***

A few hours later, I tug a fresh shirt over my head. Instinctively, I reach for the strip of condoms on my dresser, a lazy feeling convincing me to drop them again without stuffing any into my pocket.

It would be easy to chalk my reaction up to the top-notch job Goose did of sucking me off earlier, but that's never stopped me before. Maybe I'm getting too old for multiple hookups in one day, or maybe the revolving door is getting a little boring. Fuck if that isn't a terrifying thought.

Bambi's door creaks open and then clicks closed at the end of the hallway, his footsteps echoing through the house. A content feeling fills me. It's been a long ass time since anyone else has lived here. I didn't realize how much I missed the company.

I shove my phone into my pocket and slip my flip-flops on, and then go to meet Bambi in the living room. He's perched on the arm of the couch, thumbing through his phone. He also changed his clothes, trading the button-up he was wearing earlier for a tight-fitted black T-shirt and a pair of shorts that land a little higher than mid-thigh, which is the absolute correct length for shorts, and that's a hill I'll die on. No man should be wearing shorts that come below his knees.

"You look good," I say, and he startles so severely that he fumbles his phone, grappling for it and ultimately catching it just before it hits the floor.

I bite the inside of my cheek to stifle a laugh. When he straightens up, his cheeks are flaming red. I wonder if he's prone to blushing anywhere else. My eyes instinctually devour his slender body again, attempting to conjure an image of what he looks like under his clothes.

I give myself a mental shake. *No sexualizing your roommate, Ten. Bad.*

"Ready to go?" I check, and Bambi nods.

"Yeah." He licks his lips and looks me up and down quickly, the action making his cheeks turn an even darker shade of red, which I'm surprised is possible. "You look good too."

I smirk. "Thanks."

We stare at each other for one of those long seconds, neither of us seeming to know what else to say, highlighting the fact that we may have worked together the past two years, but we hardly know each other.

"So." I point my thumb in the direction of the front door, and Bambi lets out an awkward laugh, nodding and following me out.

The night is balmy as we step out the door,

not bothering to lock it behind me. The scent of the ocean touches everything, permeating every last corner of the island, seeping into it and becoming one. Even if I ever do leave—perish the thought—I'm sure everything I own would smell like the beach for the rest of my life.

I bypass my golf cart and head straight for the road on foot. I plan to get too plastered to drive it home, and Bambi doesn't protest the walk. It's not like it's far. Nothing on the island is.

"How long have you lived here?" Bambi asks as we walk, the waves crashing in the distance and the scrape of our shoes on the asphalt the only sound for miles. It's like an entirely different world tonight than it was twenty-four hours ago. There are no more wild tourists carousing in the streets, no more drunken orgies... at least not for a few more hours. You have to give the locals a little time to light the driftwood bonfire before we get sloshed enough for all that.

I give a low whistle, doing the mental math on how long it's been. "I guess it'll be seven years this month. Damn, I'm getting old."

He laughs. "You love it here." It's not a question, but there's curiosity laced in his tone.

A warm feeling spreads through my chest, painting a fresh smile on my lips. "Fuck yeah. I can't imagine living anywhere else. I'm planning to go full Harold: die right here, haunt the place.

He can handle all of the romantic shit. I'll be the island's patron saint of casual sex…although, I'll probably have to fight Easy for it."

"There's plenty of action. I'm sure you two could split it. That way, you can each get days off too," he reasons.

"Smart. No one wants to have to do ghost shit seven days a week for six months straight," I agree. "What about you? What brought you to the island?"

He's different from most of the locals. I never see him at any of the parties. I've never once heard a story about him hooking up with anyone—although we all kind of assume he has a thing going with Nacho, but that's fully unconfirmed. He's intriguing.

"Um…" He gives a huffing little laugh, tucking his hands into his pockets and kicking a stone as he walks. "Well, I was in my first year of med school at Columbia when my dad died. It kind of threw me for a loop. We were close." He pauses, the pain in his voice palpable. My heart constricts and, without thinking, I reach over and grab his hand, giving it a small squeeze for comfort.

He looks over at me, a bit startled, but he doesn't pull away. He squeezes back and goes on. "Anyway, I went through his funeral in a bit of a fog, and then, I don't know, the next thing I knew, I was on the ferry here. I barely even remember the flight from New York to South Carolina. I hardly even knew where I was headed when I realized I was on the ferry. My friends talked about the island all the time. They came for Spring Break here every year of college, but I'm not sure why it's the place I chose while I was in a fog of grief."

"The island has a strange way of doing that, drawing the people in who belong here."

"Yeah," he agrees, not sounding entirely sure. He might not be, but I am. The island always knows. I don't know how, but she does.

I realize I'm still holding his hand and drop it quickly. "Shit, sorry. I know you aren't big on being touched."

He slows his steps, coming to a full stop before I realize it. I pause and look back to find him blinking at me owlishly with those big doe eyes of his. "How...?" He licks his lips and furrows his brow.

I shrug. "I notice things."

"Oh." He ducks his head, but I notice a smile before he does. "Well, thank you. It's actually mostly strangers, though, so it's okay if you want to touch me." Bambi's cheeks instantly pink. "Not that you want to *touch* me, I just mean we're roommates, and I don't want you to think

I'm going to freak out if you accidentally brush against me in the kitchen or anything."

I chuckle. "Noted." He starts walking again, awkward tension radiating off him. "I was in med school too," I confess, although it's not the *entire* truth, in an attempt to get the comfort we were sharing a few moments ago back.

"You *were*?"

I laugh again. "Wow, I feel like I should be offended by that level of shock."

"Sorry, you just don't..."

"Seem like a doctor?" I predict the end of the sentence he left hanging, and he nods. "I guess that's why I'm not."

"What happened?"

"I got in a bad car accident, almost died."

"Oh shit," he mutters.

"Yeah, waking up in the hospital and realizing the validity of the expression *feel like you've been hit by a bus* has a way of forcing you to re-evaluate your life." I can remember the pain like it was yesterday. The sound of crunching glass and metal still haunts my dreams some nights. Luckily, the sounds of crashing waves and seagulls do a hell of a job of drowning it out.

Laughter and the roar of a fire reach our ears, alerting us that the party is nearby. I tilt my head toward the space between the two nearest houses and Bambi follows me. The sand catches in my flip-flops, weighing them down until I stop to slip them off.

Bambi does the same, banging them together to shake off the loose sand and then following me between the houses and onto the private section of beach normally reserved for the wealthy tourists who rent these places. But during the off-season, it's all ours, just like the rest of the island.

Not that having tourists here stops any of us much. They tend to have epic beach parties down here and never complain when hot locals join in on the fun.

The bonfire comes into view, flames of blue and lavender joining the yellow and orange as the salt from the ocean burns off the driftwood. The smell of smoke and sand and sea fills my lungs and sends a thrill through me. There's nothing quite like the first party of the fall.

Bambi is quiet next to me, so I bump my shoulder against his and grin when he looks at me. "Ready to have some fun?"

"As I'll ever be," he says gamely, and I bark out a laugh.

"It's a party, not a root canal. How about I grab you a beer?"

"Oh, it's okay. You don't have to babysit me or anything." He folds his arms and gives me a reassuring smile.

"It's not babysitting. I invited you out, and I'm going to go get myself a beer anyway."

"Okay. Thank you."

"No problem. I'll be right back, don't have too much fun without me," I tease.

He rolls his eyes. "I'll try not to."

BAMBI

Every resident on the island seems to be here. Boston is talking and laughing with Devil and his husband, Angel. Trick is trying to cajole Hennessey and Goose into a limbo contest. Even Raven is here, wearing his signature fishnet stockings and dark eyeliner, perched on a piece of driftwood beside Lyric, who's strumming his guitar, a lit joint dangling between his lips. Dozens of other men litter the beach: talking, drinking, laughing. The only person I don't spot is Chef Storm, but that's not surprising. He's probably the only man on this island more reclusive than I am.

I shove my hands into my pockets and kick at the sand absently, feeling all kinds of out of place. Having Nacho gone highlights the fact that I may have been here the past two years, but I haven't really *been* here. I know everyone, but

I haven't managed to make any friends, and it's *very* obvious I haven't been experiencing island life the way everyone else has. Nacho was right.

I take a deep breath, watching the flames dance and making a vow to myself. I'm going to do it right this winter. I will have a *real* off-season experience, I'm going to make friends, and if I have any say in it, I'm going to have sex. By the time spring comes, I'll be able to make a decision about my future, knowing I've given it my all here.

Ten returns with a couple of beer bottles, holding one out to me. "You look like you've relaxed a little."

I give a resolute nod, taking the drink and bringing it to my lips. The glass is ice cold from the cooler, beads of condensation making it slippery in my fingers. "You really don't need to worry about me. I'm going to mingle."

He lifts both eyebrows, smirking. "You're going to mingle, huh? Well, by all means, don't let me stop you."

Ten wanders over to where Easy, Lux, and Trick are laughing raucously, and I glance around one more time, my eyes settling on Hennessey and Goose, who are now seated near Lyric, talking and swaying to the music he's playing.

Okay, I can do this. I guzzle down half my beer to settle my nerves, and then I make my way over to them.

"Bambi." Goose gives me a dopey, drunk smile.

"Uh, hey." I take a seat.

"Are the rumors true? You and Ten?" Hennessey asks, leaning forward, his eyes sparkling with interest.

"Me and…?" I look over at Ten on the other side of the fire and laugh at the absurdity of the idea. "*No*, not like that anyway. He offered me his spare room, that's all."

"Intrigue." Raven grins, looking at me a little too long. I'm not one for all that psychic stuff, but I'd still rather he not stare at me in a way that feels like he's peering right into my soul.

"His dick is pierced," Goose says with a smirk, reaching over and snagging the joint from between Lyric's lips and putting it between his own.

My whole body heats and my cock hardens. I slip a hand onto my lap to hide the evidence of my arousal and take another long sip from my beer.

Hennessey cringes. "That has got to hurt to have done."

Goose shrugs, smoke billowing out from between his pretty bowed lips as he offers the joint to Hen. "All I know is it's fun to play with."

Hen takes it and inhales a long drag as well.

"So, did you and Nacho break up?" Lyric asks, pausing his strumming to take the joint back.

I frown, looking around at the rest of the group, trying to figure out who he's talking about. He can't mean me, can he? "We weren't together," I answer.

"You weren't?" Hen, Goose, and Raven all look at me with surprise.

"No. Did someone say we were?" Lyric offers me the joint, and I stare at it in his outstretched hand for a few seconds, feeling like I'm at my first high school party all over again. Of course, no one offered me weed back then. No one looked at me twice because they assumed I was nothing but the anti-social nerd who really didn't belong at the party. They were right.

But I *did* just decide I was going to go all in. This is all in. I take the joint from him, the skunky smell of weed tickling my nose as I bring it close. I'm coughing before it even touches my lips, but I drag in a lungful anyway. It burns all the way down my throat, and I start to cough again, harder this time, my throat and lungs feeling like they've been flayed open and lit on fire.

"Fuck," I mutter, passing the joint back to him and gulping down the rest of my beer to quench the burn.

"No one really said. I guess we all just assumed," Goose says when my coughing fit ends.

"The two of you were always together. You never hooked up with anyone else…" Hen trails off, letting the implication hang there.

I giggle, my head feeling extremely floaty all of a sudden, like it's not even attached to my body anymore. Oh my god, do I still have a body? I look down, patting myself all over just to be sure. Yup, it's still there. *Phew.*

"Me and Nacho?" I laugh again. "No, no, no, no, no."

"So, no?" Lyric teases with a smirk.

"*No,*" I say emphatically one more time. Lyric pulls a fresh joint out of his pocket. It's passed down the line again, and I take it without hesitation. It doesn't burn as much this time and I only cough a little. The giddy feeling inside me intensifies, and I start to giggle again.

I'm vaguely aware of the amused looks I'm getting from them, but I can't seem to stop. I snort, trying to catch my breath between fits of laughter.

"So, if not Nacho, are you just amazingly sneaky with your hookups? Asexual? Incredibly picky?" Hen asks once I get my laughter under control.

I glance across the fire at Ten. He throws his head back and laughs loudly at something Easy is saying.

"Interesting," Goose says.

I jerk my head back toward them, the fast movement making me dizzy and giggly all over again. I wiggle my toes in the soft sand, still warm from the sun that set a few hours ago, and I gasp.

"Oh my god, the sand feels so good." I reach down and scoop up a handful to sift through my fingers.

I'm vaguely aware of the conversation continuing around me, the murmur of voices getting lost among the cackle of the fire and the rush of the ocean several yards away. I turn and look out at the waves crashing, the moon reflecting off the water. The smell of saltwater beckons me, calling me away from the oppressive heat of the bonfire and the lingering scent of weed and booze.

My legs carry me down the beach before I even organize my thoughts to do so. The party sounds fade into the background, the ocean getting louder as I get close enough for the lukewarm water to lap at my toes, my feet sinking into the wet sand. Water rushes in, and before I know it, I'm in up to my knees.

I laugh again, more in surprise than anything. The water feels so good. I should go swimming.

I grab the bottom of my shirt and pull it over my head, swaying with the water as I wade in deeper. I drop it and don't bother to wonder where it goes. Out to sea, I suppose. I imagine a dolphin finding it. A shirt could change dolphin society. They'll all start wearing clothes and learn to walk on land. I might've just started the apocalypse all because I carelessly dropped my shirt. Well, if the apocalypse is inevitable now, I might as well let them have my pants too.

I unbutton my shorts and kick them off, along with my underwear. The sand gives under my feet, too soft for stable steps. I stumble and splash forward, gasping and sputtering as salty water fills my mouth and nose.

I try to push myself up, but another wave washes over me, knocking me back down and forcing more water down my throat. I'm contemplating a watery death—surprisingly calmly, I might add—when a pair of strong arms wraps around me and hauls me out of the ocean.

I gag and spit the water out, dragging in

breaths as the world seems to spin. Or maybe I'm the one spinning? I flail, grappling for something to grab on to. My hands manage to find a pair of very sturdy shoulders.

"Thought you'd take a little swim?" Ten asks, sounding breathless and a little tense but otherwise amused.

Ten. That's who pulled me out of the ocean and is currently holding me bridal style in his arms.

"I'm naked," I mutter, and he just chuckles.

"Come on, let's get you home."

"I can walk." I push weakly on his chest, but he doesn't put me down.

"I could use a good workout. Humor me."

The world is still swirling around me, and my eyelids are feeling a little heavy now that my heart isn't trying to beat out of my chest and my life isn't flashing before my eyes. I rest my head on his shoulder and close my eyes.

"Is he okay?" someone asks, sounding distorted and far away.

"He's fine. I'm taking him home so he can sleep it off," Ten answers. "No more illicit drugs for cute baby deer. Understood?" His voice sounds so much more menacing than I've heard before. Well, maybe once when this guy at the bar wouldn't stop harassing me, and Ten threatened to kick his ass down the street and back to the ferry because *we don't tolerate that shit around here.*

I snort a laugh at the memory.

"No more weed," someone—Lyric?—agrees.

The sway of his steps is mesmerizing, lulling me into a peaceful, not-quite-asleep yet not-quite-awake place. I curl my fingers around the front of his shirt, the other still around his neck for balance.

"My clothes are with the dolphins now," I murmur.

He laughs. "Nah, they'll wash back up on shore and make nice nest material for some seagulls."

"Oh, good." I yawn. "I don't want a dolphin apocalypse."

"No, we wouldn't want that," he agrees solemnly.

I feel like I'm being carried home by a very strong cloud that smells like sexy man and sandalwood soap. My whole body feels tingly, my cock starting to swell and throb from the amazing smell filling my lungs.

"Goose said your dick is pierced."

Ten barks out an amused sound. "A guy can't have any secrets around here, can he?" He doesn't sound upset, but I do wonder what it's like to know that most people in town have seen you naked.

A foggy, reasonable part of my brain points out that literally the entire island just saw me naked as Ten carried me away from the party. It's not so different from that semester that I stripped to cover the cost of my dorm and meal plan.

I'm surprised when Ten lowers me into my bed. How did he get the front door open while holding me? And did we get home really fast, or does time just have no meaning anymore?

"I'm going to get you some water," he says.

I mumble something I think is supposed to be *thank you* before drifting into a dreamless sleep.

CHAPTER 5

BAMBI

I'm barely even conscious before the utter horror of what I did last night washes over me. Stoned. Naked. Embarrassing near-drowning. *Ten*.

"No," I groan, grabbing one of my pillows and putting it over my face. *No more illicit drugs for cute baby deer.* Ten's words echo back through my mind, and for a second, my brain gets hung up on the word *cute.* Ten thinks I'm cute? I'm sure he doesn't mean it that way. He means cute like baby turtles are cute, not *I'd totally fuck that dude* cute.

I blindly grope for my phone, expecting to find it on the nightstand where I always leave it. This requires a call and possibly a pep talk from Nacho to convince me to ever leave this room or show my face to anyone on the island again for the rest of my life. Okay, mostly to Ten, but it's embarrassing that everyone else saw me naked and stupid too.

My fingers brush across smooth wood and

nothing more, and that's when it hits me. My phone was in my pocket last night...the pocket of the shorts that are floating somewhere in the Atlantic Ocean as we speak.

Fan-fucking-tastic.

At least I didn't have my wallet with me. Silver lining. With a few more childish groans of protest, I manage to convince myself to get out of bed, dragging my ass to the bathroom so I can take a shower in the hope that if I can get the water hot enough, it will wash away the memories of last night.

If I didn't already have thoroughly filthy feelings toward Ten, the killer water heater he installed might do it. I sigh happily when I step under the hot spray of the shower. You know, it's kind of funny when you think about it, getting high and trying to go for a swim. And it's not like everyone else on the island hasn't seen each other naked. It's practically a rite of passage.

I chuckle, the tension in my chest easing as I stick my face under the hot water. Before the whole naked part, I was actually having fun. Hen, Goose, Lyric, and Raven were being really cool, and the atmosphere was great. Plus, okay, the fact that Ten saved me from drowning and carried me all the way home is good for at *least* a year's worth of jerk-off fuel.

This is totally fine. I just need to go get a

new prepaid phone from the convenience store up the street, and I'm sure by the time the next beach party rolls around, everyone will have already forgotten the skinny-dipping incident anyway.

With that plan in place, I finish up my shower, taking a few minutes to luxuriate in the new soap I bought from Goose a few days ago: strawberry-mango. I have no clue how he gets the suds to feel so thick and rich, but the man is a soap-making genius.

Once I'm squeaky clean and have successfully worked up the nerve to face Ten, I dry off and get dressed. My hair flops over my face, well overdue for a haircut. Maybe I'll swing by Tea Bagged after I get my phone and ask Raven if he has time to give me a quick trim. Yes, he offers haircuts in his apartment directly above his tea shop. These are the ins and outs of island life, my friend.

I peek my head out of the bedroom cautiously, listening for whether Ten is up and if he's alone. Without my phone, I don't have the first clue what time it is, whether I'm up early or late, if it's morning or nearing afternoon. It leaves me feeling slightly off-kilter.

There isn't a sound coming from the rest of the house aside from the rattling sound of one of the rats drinking from their water bottle. I head down the hallway to the kitchen, which is empty and spotless, aside from a single sheet of paper sitting on the nearest counter.

It's a note from Ten.

Bambi,

When I told you to let loose and have some fun last night, I didn't mean to drown yourself. I have to give it to you though, you know how to make a night interesting. Lucky for you, no hangovers from too much weed! I'm out on a hike today and probably won't be back until later in the afternoon, but I have some killer ahi to grill up for dinner if you're around. Left some iced coffee in the refrigerator for you if that's your thing.

Catch you later,

Ten

I smile at the strange familiarity in the note, as if we've been roommates and friends for years instead of one very awkward night. I suppose I shouldn't be surprised since that particular quality caused me to develop an almost instantaneous crush on the man the day we met.

He's hot, don't get me wrong. He has more than earned his nickname, but there are plenty of drool-worthy dudes in the world. There's only a handful who can look at a lost, terrified twenty-four-year-old, who just stumbled off a ferry without so much as a suitcase to his name, and offer a friendly smile, a job application, and directions to the house of the man who rents the cheapest apartments on the island. It felt like he gave a shit, even though he didn't have a single reason to. I guess I'm a sucker for that.

I fold the note, put it in my pocket, and grab the iced coffee from the refrigerator.

The best thing about September is that it's still warm, but some of the humidity is slowly starting to let up. I take a deep breath when I step outside, reveling again at how quiet and empty the streets are.

A pelican flies by overhead, and I smile, using my hand to shield my eyes from the glare of the sun as I watch the bird disappear back in the direction of the beach. I see a few other residents going about their day as I walk down the main strip toward the convenience store. The call of seagulls and crash of the ocean waves a couple of miles away lend to the serene feeling of the late morning.

I sip my coffee and amble slowly down the street, in no particular hurry to get where I'm going.

Surprisingly, the off-season took the most

getting used to here. Normal life doesn't have a pause button like time does here on the island. It's constantly *go, go, go*, every minute until you rush all the way to an early grave. The first year I was here, I thought I'd go crazy not having anything I *needed* to do for months on end. Now, it's hard to imagine going back to the real world... unfortunately, it's also a little hard to imagine *not* eventually going back to the real world. I'm still not sure where that leaves me.

I get a new prepaid phone and pick up one of those disgustingly sweet Hostess cherry pies as well. I get a grin from the clerk, leaving no room to wonder if he saw my stoned skinny-dipping extravaganza last night. I give him a tight smile in return and hurry out of the store.

I'm about to head straight back home to open my new phone and call Nacho, maybe find something to spend the day binge-watching on the couch, when my eyes are drawn to the *one* shop in town I've never set foot inside.

Heavenly Toys, owned by Angel, *obviously*.

My stomach squirms as I find myself rooted to the spot. I've never had a particular desire to go into the sex toy shop. Okay, that's not entirely true. I *have* thought about it from time to time. I've just never quite worked up the courage.

I chew on my bottom lip, staring at the sign in the window declaring that there are "*Dil-*

dos of every size and shape, flavored lube, buckets of lube, SO. MUCH. LUBE. Vibrators, outfits...the best Palm Island has to offer. What are you waiting for?"

Well, what *am* I waiting for? I'm an adult. I can own a sex toy. My cock aches at the thought, my hole clenching. I've played with myself, teasing my fingers outside my hole, but I've always wondered what it would feel like to be *really* full.

I swallow, dragging in a shivery breath. I promised myself last night that I would dive into this whole thing with both feet, and sex is a big part of that. Who said it had to be sex with another person? After all, it's hard to imagine getting down and dirty with any of the other locals aside from Ten, and since Ten is very likely not an option, I need to get creative if I'm going to uphold this particular promise to myself.

Holding my head up high, I cross the street and push the door to the shop open. The bell over the door jangles. The smell of plastic and lube, just barely covered by the scent of incense, tickles my nose.

A blond head pops up from behind one of the far shelves, Angel's curly hair bobbing with the movement. His eyes widen when he sees me, and then a welcoming smile spreads over his face.

"Bambi, hey. How are you feeling?"

Ugh. I guess I'd better get used to this for at least the next few days.

I put on my bravest smile and force a laugh. "At least weed doesn't cause a hangover," I echo Ten's note, and Angel chuckles in agreement.

"Amen. Can I help you find anything? Dildo? Jerk sleeves? Lube? Condoms?" he rattles off a few options, and my cheeks heat up. This was a huge mistake.

"Oh, uh..."

"Or I can leave you alone to browse by yourself? You can just give me a shout if you have any questions."

"Yes, that would be great."

He nods and disappears behind the shelf, leaving me to be intimidated all on my own. Awesome.

I gravitate in the direction of the anal toys, feeling like even more of a virgin than I am as I try to decipher what each one is used for. The rubbery cocks I get. But what in the hell are the jewel-ended things? And *why* would I want something that requires an app to use?

Best to keep it simple. I focus on the wall of dildos. Traditional, yes, but still intimidating. They're organized not only by size but firmness.

How firm do I want a dildo? I'm certainly *not* about to ask Angel that.

I'm about to turn around and walk out, considering this a total bust and going back to my original TV and couch plan.

"Not that one."

A voice from behind me startles me. I look over my shoulder to find Hennessey with a friendly grin, dressed in a tight, blue T-shirt that highlights his slim, petite frame and the colorful dragon tattoos on his arms.

"I'm sorry?"

"That dildo you're eyeing is *way* too big," he advises. "Unless I'm reading our conversation from last night completely wrong."

"Well, um…" Did he totally peg me as a virgin? No way. No one ever does because adult virgins are apparently unicorns. Go me.

"This one, sweetie." He reaches around me and picks up the moderately sized, semi-firm cock from the wall.

I have to give it to him. It *is* less intimidating than the others, so it's probably a good place to start.

"Thanks." I take it from him, my thumb brushing over the silky texture of the toy through the little *feel me* window in the plastic box. My cock twitches, and I clear my throat.

"Ah, that's what I was looking for." He plucks another toy off the wall that, according to the package, has *real thrusting action*. "Angel," he calls out, causing the man to pop back up like a gopher.

"Henny, how are you doing, sweetness?"

"Perfect. Just need you to ring me up."

Hen and Angel both head in the direction of the cash register, and I sort of trail behind like a lost little puppy...a lost little puppy clutching a dildo.

Hennessey pays for his toy, but he doesn't immediately leave the shop, instead lingering near the register as if he's waiting for me. I fumble with my wallet, my cheeks flaming again as I make my purchase, trying not to melt into a puddle of embarrassment when Angel winks and tells me to enjoy.

"Thanks," I mumble.

"Let's grab some tea," Hen says, looping an arm through mine and leading me out of the shop before I can even think about begging off.

Tea Bagged, the café-slash-palm and tarot reading-slash-occasional barbershop, is located only a few buildings down from Angel's. I stuff the bag from Heavenly Toys inside my other bag to hide the logo. I'm an adult and a med student—if I ever go back to school—and I'm fully aware that it's healthy and normal to masturbate. Everyone does it blah, blah, blah. I just don't want everyone in town knowing I bought a dildo. I've suffered enough embarrassment for one week, thank you very much.

Hennessey pushes open the door to the café, a wind chime in place of a regular bell.

"Hen and Bambi!" Raven calls our names from somewhere unseen.

I look around, half-expecting to find the strange man hanging from the ceiling, or at the very least evidence of a camera he must be watching us from. I don't see anything other than some cobwebs in the corners of the ceiling and the cute little chandeliers that hang over each table.

"Where is—"

Before I can finish getting my question out, Raven stumbles out of the back room, his arms weighed down with plastic pumpkins and fake crows. He has a big smile on his face, his lips done up with black lipstick, a touch of glitter on his cheeks, and as always, wearing his signature black shorts and fishnets.

"Halloween decorations already?" Hen asks, arching an eyebrow at him.

"It's *never* too soon. You're saving the date

for my annual Samhain party, right?" He looks at Hen first and then at me.

"Your costume party, right?" Hen checks.

"Duh," he says cheekily, dumping the plastic decor onto the nearest table.

"I'll be there," Hen promises, and then they both turn toward me.

"Oh, um, yeah, maybe." I've always loved Halloween, and I've never turned down a costume party, but ever since my dad died, it hasn't really been the same. Besides, I'm sure they're just being polite.

Raven stares at me for a few uncomfortable seconds, his eyes feeling like they're looking straight into my soul.

"You'll be here. And your costume looks *super* cute," he says confidently. "Have a seat. You guys want coffee or tea?"

He waves at all the open tables, and Hen and I sit. I set my bag down and then anxiously change my mind and slip it under my chair instead. Raven chuckles.

"I just looked into the future, Bambi. You think I don't already know what's in that bag?"

Hen rolls his eyes. "Ugh, with the psychic schtick already."

"It's not a schtick," Raven sniffs.

"Oh yeah? Answer me this then…" Instead of asking anything aloud, Hen simply looks at Raven with an intense gaze.

Raven smirks, leaning in close as if he's going to tell a secret. "Only on Tuesdays," he stage whispers an answer to the unasked question, shooting me a wink when Hen starts to chuckle.

He straightens up and turns toward the counter area. "Sit tight, boys. Drinks are on the way."

"We didn't even tell you what we want yet," Hen points out.

Raven scoffs and returns the playful eye roll. Their banter and teasing put me at ease. I lean forward with my elbows on the table, smiling as a happy feeling of belonging fills my chest.

Maybe Nacho is right. I haven't given everyone else here enough of a chance.

TEN

"Heads-up," Easy warns, ducking a low-hanging branch. I do the same, brushing off the spider web that clings to my face as I pass it.

The trail is getting to be overgrown, tall grasses catching on my hiking boots as we make our way up the side of the small mountain. The main trail is well-kept for tourists, but the rest are hit or miss, mostly miss. That's okay. Easy and I prefer to rough it out anyway.

The heat of the day slows us both down, but we're not in any kind of a rush to make it to the top. I wonder if Bambi found the note I left him and if he enjoyed the iced coffee. I smile, remembering how funny he was last night, even if he did nearly give me a heart attack when he disappeared under the waves for a minute.

Easy slows near a rock outcropping with a view that looks out over the ocean.

"Let's sit and enjoy the scenery for a bit," I suggest, whipping my shirt off to wipe the sweat from my face and then fishing my water bottle out of my pack. I gulp some down and hand it over to Easy, who does the same before sitting with his legs dangling over the edge.

I take a deep breath, filling my lungs with the green scent of all the plants around us, letting the seemingly endless expanse of the ocean replenish the sense of peace inside me. "Are you starting to get bored with the casual sex thing yet?"

"Bite your tongue," Easy gasps. "Better yet, bite someone else's tongue." He gives me a cheeky smirk.

I snort. "I never thought I'd say it either,

man. Don't get me wrong, I love sex. I love that rush of a first connection, the thrill of making someone gasp and moan for me." He hums in agreement, shamelessly adjusting his cock in his shorts. "But I swear to fuck I can't have sex with you again."

He cackles. "Hard agree. But I'm not the only other guy on the island."

"Yeah," I sigh. "But I don't really want to hook up with Hen or Boston or find my way into another three-way with Angel and Devil either." I list off the usual suspects. "We need some fresh meat around here."

"Bambi's meat was looking pretty fresh last night." He waggles his eyebrows and, to my surprise, a tight, hot feeling squeezes my chest. Before I know what I'm doing, I shove his shoulder, a sound I can only describe as a growl rumbling through my throat.

"Dude, what the fuck?" He grips the rock and shoves me back.

"He didn't mean to show everyone his dick. Don't talk about it like that."

"Whoa, chill. I was making a joke. What's your problem?" He eyes me curiously.

"Shit, I don't know. Sorry, that was fucked up to push you when you're right on the ledge like that."

A smirk twists his lips. "Relax, I swear I won't look at Bambi's dick again. He's all yours."

I frown. All mine? What the fuck is Easy talking about? I shake that question off and try to get back on track.

"So, you really never wonder what it would be like to find someone more…permanent?"

"I already have someone permanent. I just don't have sex with him," he says.

I guess he's right. What he has with Lux is a hell of a lot more permanent than most romantic relationships I've seen. How many other straight dudes would follow their best friend to a gay resort island to build a life and a business?

We enjoy the view for a few more minutes before we get moving again, taking our time, in no hurry to be anywhere but out here. Easy picks a few flowers and puts them into his hair with a flourish, attracting honeybees as we walk.

By the time we part ways back in town a few hours later, I'm drenched in sweat, my shirt draped over my shoulder, my skin bronzed from the sun. My thighs and calves ache from too many months stuck behind the bar, slinging drinks until the wee hours every morning before stumbling into bed with a willing tourist and doing it all over again the next night.

Maybe Easy is right. Who could complain

about a life like that? Except, lately, I've been wondering if perhaps it's time for something more. What that is, I don't have the first clue.

I jog up the back steps to my place, going in through the double doors on the deck. A grin jumps to my lips when I step inside to see Bambi's flip-flops in a heap inside the door, casually cast off on his way into the house at some point. I didn't realize how much I missed having a roommate, not having to come home to an empty house every night. I guess Bambi is doing me just as much of a favor as I'm doing him.

"Ten?" his voice comes from the kitchen, just a hint of that sweet shyness that intrigued me the first night we met, as if I was some kind of celebrity he wasn't sure he was allowed to talk to.

I snort at the memory, shaking my head before going toward the sound of his voice. "Yeah?"

I find him standing in front of the open refrigerator. "Oh, good. I was just wondering if I should thaw the fish for you so it would be ready to cook by the time you got home. But then I wasn't sure when you'd be back, and I didn't want to thaw it *too* early and ruin it."

While he rambles, I crowd in and reach around him to pull the ahi out. He goes still as my body flattens against his. *Fuck.* I jerk back, giving him his space.

"Shit, sorry. The guys always tell me I have no sense of personal space. I didn't mean to make you uncomfortable."

"Oh, no, you're fine." His cheeks are pink, his hands shoved into his pockets now as he slips out from between me and the refrigerator.

"Are you going to stay and eat with me?" I call after him before he can make it out of the kitchen. He stutters to a stop.

"Sure, if you want me to."

"Of course I do, roomie." I smile at him, grabbing the fish and closing the refrigerator. It actually feels like they've thawed enough, so I step outside to light the grill and then get started on mixing my signature dry rub.

"So, you went hiking?" he asks, sitting on the edge of the table while he watches me prepare dinner.

"Yeah. Easy and I took the north trail up to the top, checked out the view for a while," I answer. "What about you? Did you get out a bit today?"

His face turns deep scarlet, and he drops his eyes from mine. Interesting. I wonder where he went. Maybe he slipped away for a hookup. But why would that be embarrassing? It only takes him a few seconds to compose himself and answer the question.

"I had to get a new phone. That merpeople civilization is about to have a technological revolution," he tsks, and I chuckle.

"I think you were worried about dolphins," I correct him.

"Was I? Well, I'm not sure if that's more or less concerning than human technology and pants in the hands of merpeople."

"It's a toss-up." I grin.

"Anyway, after that, I ran into Hen, and we got tea and hung out for a little while," he finishes.

"Oh yeah? I didn't know you and Hen were tight." I put the steaks on a plate, and Bambi jumps up to get the door for me so I can toss the meat on the grill.

"Not really. We just sort of started talking, becoming friends, whatever," he says when I step back inside.

"Cool. He's pretty chill. We might have to coordinate to make sure he and Easy don't end up in the house at the same time, though, because that would more than likely lead to bloodshed," I warn, cringing at the carnage that would ensue if we accidentally had them here together.

"Why?" he asks, resuming his spot on the table while I grab a water bottle out of the refrigerator, downing half of it to replace the sweat the hike rung out of me today.

"Why?" I laugh, using the back of my hand to wipe my mouth. "Haven't you seen the *Fuck Easy* sign that Hen paints every month? He hates Easy."

Bambi shakes his head. "I guess I haven't been too plugged in. I only got here…"

"Two years ago," I finish for him, and he frowns.

"Damn, okay, yeah, I have no excuse, I guess. Hen got here after I did, didn't he?"

"He was a tourist who stayed after the season. You'd have to ask him about the rest because I only ever got Easy's side of the story, and I'm sure that was creative history, to say the least."

He laughs. "Okay. Well, I'll make sure to give you a heads-up if he's coming to hang out. Although, I doubt he will." He tugs his bottom lip between his teeth, those big eyes all doe-like. I don't know what it is about those eyes of his. I wonder if he notices how quickly I jump to make drinks for him or do just about anything else he asks for at the bar when he turns those eyes of his on me.

"Do you like to hike or anything?" I ask.

"No. I actually haven't explored the island much," he confesses, and I gasp at that blasphemy.

"This is the happiest place on Earth."

"I'm pretty sure that's Disneyland," he argues.

"Hmm, gay resort island complete with natural beauty, any water sport you can imagine, and an endless buffet of blowjobs and casual sex versus some shitty roller coasters?"

Bambi cackles. "Apparently, I've been doing this island *completely* wrong."

"Lucky for you, you're with me now." I smirk at him, and his cheeks pink again, his eyes locking on mine for a minute.

"Yeah, I guess so. We can go hiking, as long as you understand that I'm likely to get winded embarrassingly quick," he warns.

"It's all about building your stamina." I shoot him another wink just because I'm dying to see his eyes widen and his cheeks flush again. I laugh when he does exactly that.

Damn, he's going to be fun to live with.

CHAPTER 6

BAMBI

I lie in my bed, the sheets and my skin warm from the morning sun streaming in through the window, trying to convince myself that it's remotely worth getting out of bed today. The only thing mildly enticing me is the fact that I told Hennessey I'd go to the beach with him and Goose. But that's not for hours, which is making me lazy.

The remnants of a dirty dream I was having cling to the edges of my subconscious and make my cock hard, which isn't helping my motivation either. I reach beneath the covers and slowly stroke myself.

The dildo I bought a few days ago jumps to my mind, hidden in the bag I stuffed under the bed when I got home. My stomach squirms and heats at the idea of pulling it out to play with it. I'm not sure if I'm ready, but maybe I could at least *look* at it.

I pull my hand off my cock long enough to roll onto my belly and reach under the bed.

My fingers quickly catch on the plastic bag, and I drag it closer. My cock is sandwiched between my body and the mattress, getting harder by the second as I fumble with the packaging to free the toy.

When I finally get it out, my breath catches at how silky smooth the material is. It feels like a real cock...not that I've touched one other than my own. With the dildo clutched in my fist, I roll to my back again, wrapping my free hand around my cock.

My memory conjures the feeling of Ten's body pressed against mine as he reached around me to get the ahi the other night. He thought he upset me, but I couldn't correct him because that would mean admitting that I was so turned on I probably could have come in my pants if he'd stayed where he was another minute or two.

My cock jerks in my fist, and I clutch the dildo tighter as well, absently dragging my thumb over the head of the toy, wondering what Ten's dick looks like. Was Goose telling the truth about him having a piercing? That nearly short circuits my brain. I put the dildo against my cock and bite back a gasp, needing to stay quiet in case these walls are thin. My heart thunders at the thought of Ten hearing me jerk off.

I pant, my toes curling as I thrust, the solid weight of the toy on my cock. I wrap my fingers around both at once, the pressure of it making my eyes roll back and my body jolt.

"Fuck," I mutter, my body trembling and tensing as my balls constrict and I spurt cum all over the toy. I fuck against it as my cock pulses, my release making things slippery, prolonging the pleasure as I clench my teeth to stay quiet and thrash on the bed.

When it's over, I slump on the bed, still breathing heavily, about ready to write both Angel and Hen personal thank you notes. You know, if thanking someone for an orgasm wasn't incredibly embarrassing. Actually, in that case, I'd have to thank Ten too, and then I'd have to dig a hole and bury myself in it. So thank you notes are off the to-do list.

I snag my shirt from yesterday off the floor and hastily clean myself and the dildo, dropping it, along with the shirt, onto my bed. I roll out of bed, feeling more invigorated and ready to greet the day. Who knew morning orgasms were better than coffee? Well, I'm guessing Easy, Ten, and Trick knew, considering how often they all get laid...and Goose, probably Hen...pretty much everyone except for me.

I grab my boxers off the floor and slip them on. When I step into the bathroom, I realize my dirty towel from yesterday is missing, leaving me without one. Hopefully, Ten has extra towels.

I open my bedroom door, ready to go in search of him, but there's no need.

Ten is standing there, one hand raised as if just about to knock, a folded towel in his other. He smiles. "I was just coming to give you this. I grabbed yours yesterday when I was doing laundry."

"Thanks." I take the towel, my heart going wild. Can he smell sweat and cum on me? Did he hear me jerking off? His eyes glance past me, landing on the bed for a fraction of a second before returning to me.

"Yeah, anyway, I'm going to start the coffee." He points over his shoulder and then turns and ambles back down the hallway, out of sight.

TEN

"Seriously," I growl down at my tented shorts. How long is an erection supposed to persist before it's a problem? For fuck's sake, it was just a dildo. I've seen dildos. I've *used* dildos. So Bambi has a dildo. My cock jerks. Okay, I need to stop thinking that word already.

I run my hand over my face and chuckle at myself. It's only been a few days since I've gotten any action, and I'm already cracking up. It's going to be a *long* off-season at this rate, but even that knowledge doesn't make anyone on the island seem any more appealing than they did yesterday. Well, except maybe…

The sound of Bambi's bedroom door opening and closing down the hall makes me jump. I laugh at myself one more time and press the button on the coffee maker.

"Coffee will be ready in a couple of minutes," I announce as soon as he appears in the kitchen.

"Thanks. I need it," he says with a yawn.

"Not a morning person?" I ask, temporarily forgetting the situation in my shorts as I turn around to face him and lean on the counter. Bambi's eyes drop, and his cheeks turn that painfully endearing shade of pink before he quickly fixes his attention on my face again.

I'm sure I should be embarrassed by being caught with an unexpected boner in my mid-thirties—I mean, that shit is supposed to end after high school, right?—but his reaction makes it hard to feel anything other than heated amusement.

"I…um…what was the question?"

I smirk, my skin prickling and my cock swelling a little more. The barbells lining my shaft rubbing and catching on the fabric of my underwear only make the situation worse.

"Not a morning person?" I repeat, mesmerized by the way his pink tongue darts out to wet his lips.

"Oh, I used to be, but it always takes me a while after the season ends to get back into a normal sleeping pattern," he answers.

"Tell me about it. By the time I'm back to normal human sleeping hours, the tourists all come back, and I'm fucked up all over again."

He laughs and nods.

I push off the counter, and my whole body aches a bit, reminding me that I haven't done my morning yoga yet. Sometimes I try to convince myself that all of these aches and pains are remnants of the accident, but I think the truth is that I'm just not twenty anymore. Yoga definitely helps. And I'll happily take the pain in exchange for hiking, surfing, and whatever else I find to amuse myself with.

"You don't mind me doing yoga in the living room, do you? I could do it in my room, but I love to open the French doors to the patio to let the ocean air in."

"I don't mind," Bambi says, his attention still fixed on my face even though my cock is finally starting to stand down. The bulge in my shorts is entirely reasonable now.

The blush in his cheeks is gone, but I can't

resist one last chance to tease him. "Great. I do it in the nude. I hope that's okay."

There it is. His cheeks flame crimson, and his eyes go wide. "I...uh...that's...um..."

I cackle. "Just fucking with you, Bambi." I shoot him a wink, and he makes a weak sound of amusement that's cute as hell.

I head into the living room with a smile plastered on my face, stopping to give treats to each of my boys before opening the patio doors and taking a deep inhale of the late-morning air. It fills me up, invigorating me from the inside out, another incredible reminder that I'm here, I'm alive, and nothing beats that.

I grab my yoga mat out of the corner and unroll it in the middle of the floor. I go through my morning routine, stretching and breathing in the energy from the ocean. Some mornings I go straight to the source, heading down to the beach to do yoga in the sand, usually naked, but if I admit that to Bambi, he might just spontaneously combust from embarrassment.

I smile to myself again in amusement, a surge of affection going through me for my new roommate.

I'm getting a deep stretch in with a downward dog when he walks into the living room, stumbling over his own feet before catching himself on the couch. I drop my head so I can look at him from between my legs.

"What's up, buttercup?"

There's that adorable blush again. Is it weird that I'm quickly becoming addicted to it? For some reason, Easy's coy remarks yesterday prickle under my skin, but I shove them away.

"I just wanted to say thanks for the coffee." He holds up a travel mug. "I'm heading down to the south beach, so I'll be back later."

"Cool. I'm probably going to hit the waves for a bit and then go to Boston's for our weekly poker night. Feel free to swing by later if you want." I'm not sure why I make the offer, but as soon as I do, I love the idea of having Bambi there, seeing how many times I can make him blush in one night, getting him out of his shell as he gets to know the guys better.

Easy's comment about Bambi's *meat* pops into my head, and I grit my teeth, a growl rumbling through my throat without my permission like I'm some sort of junkyard dog with a bone. What the fuck is wrong with me?

"Oh, uh, maybe."

"I'll text you his address. That way if you decide to come by, you can."

He nods, and I catch myself smiling again.

It's nice to have a roommate.

CHAPTER 7

BAMBI

I spend the entire walk down to the south beach trying to get the image of Ten's dick bulge out of my mind. The thick, hard outline pressed against the thin fabric of his pajama pants... yeah, it's not working.

I groan at myself even as a very slutty, repressed part of my brain floats the idea that Ten doesn't seem terribly picky about who he hooks up with, so why not me? No, I can't lose my virginity like that...can I? No, right? Or...okay, *maybe*.

By the time my feet hit sand, I still haven't worked my way around to a conclusion about whether or not I could fall into bed with Ten given half the chance. Knowing me, I would get a stress nosebleed like I used to when I was a kid. Nothing sexier than sneezing blood all over a guy's dick when you try to go down on him. I'm sure it happens to guys like Goose all the time.

A bitter taste fills my mouth at the reminder that they've hooked up. Ugh, why am

I even bothering to think about this? Ten has never once shown the slightest bit of interest in me.

"Bambi." Hen waves at me from down by the water as if I could miss him and Goose, literally the only two people on the beach right now.

I head straight for them, my feet sinking into the hot sand. "Hey, guys," I greet when I reach them, kicking off my shoes and plopping my ass down in the sand next to them.

Goose looks at my travel mug and grins, reaching into the large pocket of his cargo shorts and pulling out a small bottle of Kahlua. "Want some?"

"I'm good, thanks."

"Probably best without Ten here to save you from drowning," Hen teases, making my face heat.

"That was hot. He's usually so chill, but you should have seen his face when he saw you go under that wave. I thought about flinging myself into the ocean to see if I could get the same treatment," Goose says, fanning himself dramatically.

I'm only vaguely aware of the second part of that sentence. Goose can fling himself wherever he likes, but what did he say about Ten's face?

"He um...what?" I pick a pretty pink shell out of the sand and put it in my pocket. "What was his face like?" That sounded casual, right?

Goose and Hen trade a grin. "It was like he was ready to fight the ocean itself to rescue a *cute baby deer*."

The two of them cackle, and my stomach dances with feelings I can't put words to.

"He probably would've done it for anyone," I mumble, absently dragging my finger through the sand to draw big, looping circles.

"Maybe," Hen says with a shrug, not sounding entirely convinced.

"I told you, we're not hooking up. We're just roommates." My mouth goes dry, saying it as if the alternative is a possibility.

"Do you think it would make things too weird to fuck when you live together?" Goose guesses.

"I feel like Ten would be super chill about it," Hennessey says. "After all, we all kind of live together, even if it's not under the same roof. Have you hooked up with any of the other locals?"

I give a sharp shake of my head and then take a hasty gulp of my coffee, not particularly wanting to throw out the big confession of my virginal status, even if it kind of seems like Hen might have already guessed.

"I wish I hadn't," Hen mutters, taking a sip from his own—I assume Kahlua-spiked—coffee. "Not Ten," he hurries to add. "I mean, I kissed Ten once, but we didn't fuck. I wasn't talking about him though."

"You know, he's not that bad of a guy if you'd just—" Goose starts to reason.

"Fuck Easy," is Hen's response.

Goose sighs but lets the topic go. Down the beach, I spot Mr. Tubbs, a large Maine coon who appeared somewhat mysteriously on the island, not belonging to anyone in particular. He's carrying a skimpy pair of blue underwear in his mouth. The guys both follow my gaze, laughing as we all start to speculate about who's going to be missing underwear later and which resident will be getting the present left on their doorstep by the strange cat.

The three of us talk and gossip for a while. Well, the two of them gossip, and I soak in all the information about everyone else on the island. I feel like the greatest soap opera of all time has been going on around me all this time without me noticing. Apparently, Angel and Devil are super into threesomes with tourists and locals alike. Boston is liable to punch Trick if he beds one more dude Boston has his eye on. And then there's something about donuts that I do *not* understand, but the two of them laugh about repeatedly.

"It's hot. Let's go swimming," Goose says after a while.

I'm about to say that I didn't bring my swimsuit when he stands up and drops his shorts right there, standing completely bare-assed in broad daylight. Okay then. His shirt follows, and Hennessey gets to his feet to do the same.

"Come on, Bambi," Hen encourages.

I guess they *have* already seen me naked. Plus, it's not like I have a particular issue with nudity. It's more about unwanted objectification, but that doesn't feel like it will be a problem. I get to my feet and join them in making a pile of my clothing. The sun on my bare skin feels invigorating but not as invigorating as the ocean as the three of us splash into the relatively calm water.

Goose disappears under the water, re-emerging a moment later, his colorful hair dark now. He slicks it back with his hands and then wipes the water droplets from his face as best he can.

"We should've gone to the waterfall instead. It's so much better than swimming in the saltwater," he says.

"The waterfall?" I ask.

They both look at me like I've lost my mind.

"You know, the *waterfall*," Hen says.

"I didn't know there was a waterfall."

"How long have you been living here, sweetie?" Goose laughs.

The question draws me up short as I realize that I haven't ever considered myself to be *living* here, only visiting. Even still, I've missed so much of what's been going on around me.

I made a jackass of myself the other night at the party, but that doesn't change the fact that I need to give the island life a real shot if I'm going to figure out why I'm here and what comes next.

"I'm thinking of going to Boston's later for this poker thing. Do you guys want to come?"

TEN

"I hope you're ready to lose some money," Boston taunts as soon as he opens his front door to me.

"I thought we were playing strip poker," I tease with a smirk.

"If a single item of clothing is shed, I'm going home," Storm calls from just inside.

"You heard the man. We can't lose the chef, or we'll be stuck with nothing but chips and beer," Boston reasons with a shrug.

"I'm not cooking," Storm says flatly, and I laugh as I step inside. The prickly chef is probably the only dude on the island who rivals me in number of tattoos, but that's where the similarities between the two of us end. Poker nights are about the only social event he can be found at.

"If he's not going to cook either way, feel free to get naked if the mood strikes," Boston jokes.

It looks like I'm the last person here. All the guys are already seated around the poker table in Boston's living room, stacks of poker chips in front of each of them. I'm surprised to see Trick seated next to Easy.

"He showed up with Easy and Lux, and he refuses to leave," Boston explains.

"Way to make a guy feel welcome," Trick complains.

"You're *not* welcome," Boston huffs, which only seems to amuse Trick.

"Rude," Trick tsks, and Boston's jaw clenches.

Oh goodie, we might get front row seats to a good old-fashioned brawl before the evening is over. Hopefully not until after I win some money from these suckers though.

I crack my knuckles and snag the last free chair. "No Devil or Raven?" I ask, looking around the table and realizing we're short a few regulars.

"I invited them. They both made vague excuses. Fuck if I know." He counts out my set of chips and pushes them across the table to me.

Easy grins and makes bed-creaking noises, laughter tittering around the table.

"I doubt it. Raven is always super weird around Angel and Devil," Trick argues, and Boston frowns, sending a deadly glare in his direction. Possibly because he had his eye on Raven a few months back, but Trick got there first? Not sure why Boston has it in his head that he can't fuck anyone Trick has been with. On a small island like this, that's seriously limiting.

"Maybe he's weird around them because they're doing the dirty," I suggest.

Storm sighs. "Are we here to gossip, or are we here to play cards?"

"Oh, honey, you know we're more than capable of both." Easy presses a sloppy kiss to Storm's cheek, earning a deep growl and an even harsher scowl while we all laugh again.

Storm uses the back of his hand to wipe the wet spot off his cheek while Boston deals the cards.

A few rounds in and Storm has already caved and started ducking into the kitchen to make appetizers in between hands, Trick keeps casually needling Boston until the vein in the poor man's forehead is throbbing, and Easy is down enough chips that I'm sure he's going to get on the strip poker bandwagon any second. So, basically, it's a typical poker night.

We're halfway through a tray of something bacon-wrapped that is literally better than sex, Easy's shirt has been discarded to somewhere unknown, and my pile of chips has grown handsomely when there's a tentative knock at the door.

We all trade curious looks, trying to figure out who it could be when most everyone Boston talks to is already here.

"Maybe Raven or Devil changed their mind?" Lux guesses.

"Whoever it is, we know it's not a booty call," Trick taunts, and Boston's jaw ticks. Maybe we should start laying bets on whether Trick will leave here with a black eye tonight.

"Only one way to find out." I lay my cards face down and push my chair back, crossing the room to the door. I pull it open, and a smile immediately jumps to my face. "Bambi."

"Hi. I, uh, you said I should come." He fidgets and then points at Hen and Goose standing behind him, both grinning like a cat with a canary. "I hope it's okay that I invited them."

"Of course." I'm not sure why I'm feeling quite so giddy that he actually showed. Maybe because I didn't expect him to? Or maybe because it feels good to finally be pulling him out of his shell.

"So, can we come in?" Hennessey takes a step closer, putting his chin on Bambi's shoulder and batting his eyelashes at me.

"Hmm," I tease them with a mock frown. "I'm not sure. Do you guys know the password?"

Someone from inside the house snorts a laugh at me. I'm not sure who because I can't seem to tear my attention off the way Bambi's already doe eyes go even wider.

"My god, you are an insufferable flirt," Goose says, and I swear I can *hear* him rolling his eyes, even if I can't seem to look anywhere but my roommate as he starts to blush crimson under my attention.

"Nope, that's not the password."

"Would you just let them in already? You're letting bugs and shit inside," Boston barks.

"I guess that's the password." I step aside to let the three of them in. "We got drinks, snacks, and if you wait a few minutes, Boston can deal you in for the next hand."

"We're out of chairs, but my lap is free," Easy flirts. Hen makes a gagging noise while Goose saunters over and helps himself to the snack tray, and Bambi gives me an uncertain look. That same hot, weirdly aggressive feeling rises inside me again, and I bite back a growl at the thought of Bambi in Easy's lap, Easy's greedy hands all over him.

Without giving it a second thought, I plop back down in my seat and drag Bambi onto my lap. His breath hitches and the soft sound that I doubt anyone else can hear is even more intriguing than his mesmerizing blush.

I put a hand on his hip to keep him steady, perched on my thighs. His T-shirt rides up just enough that my thumb accidentally brushes over his warm, smooth skin. My cock swells, and I have to shift to keep Bambi from feeling the results of yet another spontaneous erection. Two in one day, what am I, thirteen again?

"Chef?" Hen sounds surprised as Storm steps back into the room from the kitchen, a smile forming on his full lips as he cocks his head at the ornery man. Hennessey works for Storm during the tourist season, so I'd say he knows him better than most of us do. Storm's lips twitch in what I can only assume is meant to be a return grin.

"Dude, we're still waiting on your bid." Trick nudges Storm's chair toward him.

He takes a seat, and the game gets back on track.

"I can stand," Bambi offers, making a move to get up as I use my free hand to pick my cards back up.

I tighten my grip on his hip to keep him from going anywhere.

I'm looking right at my cards, but I'm not paying any attention to them by the time it gets around to my turn. Fuck it, I push all my chips into the pot in the middle of the table just to enjoy everyone's outrage at me going all in.

There's nothing like poker night.

CHAPTER 8

BAMBI

Popcorn. *Check*. Giant bag of Twizzlers. *Check*. Queue full of all my favorite horror movies. *Check*. Perfect Friday night. *Check*.

I get Fred and Barney out of their cage, setting them both down on the back of the couch and giving them a piece of popcorn each. They're ridiculously cute, using their little hands to hold their treats, nibbling them happily while I get comfortable on the couch.

I'm trying not to listen too hard to the sounds of Ten getting ready to go out for the night. Is he going to hook up with someone? Not that it's any of my business. He hasn't had anyone to the house in the two weeks since I moved in, but that doesn't mean he's not seeing anyone. It's Ten, after all. He could have anyone he wants…and has as far as I can tell. And I don't just mean because he's the definition of sexy. He has this way of looking at you that makes you feel like the only person in the room.

A little shiver runs down my spine just

thinking about that piercing gaze of his, that look that just...*lingers* until I feel hot all over. And I do mean *all* over. I lick my lips and shift to adjust my swelling erection before it becomes uncomfortable.

Ten's footsteps in the hallway make me feel jittery. I roll my eyes inwardly at myself. You'd think after two weeks of living together, some of my reactions to him would start to chill. If anything, I'm *more* nervous around him now than ever.

"Party at Raven's tonight, Bambi," he announces when he steps into the living room, wearing a tight white T-shirt and a pair of jeans that hug...*places*. My throat goes dry, and I can feel my face heating. Even if I couldn't feel it, Ten's cocky smirk would be a dead giveaway that I'm blushing like a virgin at an orgy. Which is way too accurate of a metaphor for comfort.

An expectant look comes over his face, and I realize there was an implied invitation in his statement.

I look at the television, *The Craft* already pulled up, waiting for me to press play, and then at the rats playfully chasing each other back and forth on the back of the couch. "I think I'm going to stay in tonight."

I would give myself an A-plus for how social I've been lately. I haven't turned down a single invitation from Ten, Hen, or Goose.

"To watch a movie?" He frowns as if he's never experienced the utter joy of holing up in the house, binge-watching movies and stuffing your face with snacks.

"To watch *three* movies," I correct. "Maybe four if the snacks don't run out first." He still doesn't seem to fully understand. "It's spooky season, so a horror movie night felt right."

"It's mid-September."

I nod gravely. "I know. I'm already two weeks behind."

He snorts a laugh, seeming to contemplate the scene before him for a few more seconds. I'm expecting him to say some nicety about having a good night and then take off for his evening of debauchery. Instead, he toes off his shoes and plops down on the couch next to me.

"*The Craft?*" he asks, grabbing a handful of popcorn and putting his feet on the coffee table.

"Teen witches going mad with power, you really can't go wrong. You know, I *was* planning to do The Craft, The Shining, Carrie, and Scream tonight, but maybe we should stick with a strictly witchy theme and watch *Hocus Pocus*, *Teen Witch*, and *Practical Magic*."

"I haven't seen a single one of the movies you just mentioned, so I'm good with whatever."

"What?" Now it's my turn to stare, dumbfounded by what I'm hearing. "You've never seen *any* of these classics?" I immediately start adding about two dozen more Halloween classics to my mental list.

Ten shrugs. "I'm not much of a movie guy, but I'm game. Put it on."

"Your life is about to change," I warn, grinning as I put the bowl of popcorn between us and offer him some of my candy.

"I'm ready," he replies solemnly, both of us chuckling as I hit play.

I'm tense and jittery the first twenty minutes of the movie, feeling like I should've insisted Ten go to the party so I could've enjoyed my movie night without all of these hot, squirmy feelings I can never shake when he's around.

But then, he starts really getting into it, laughing and asking questions, making guesses about what's going to happen, and I find myself relaxing. Well, as relaxed as I can be with the scent of whiskey soap on Ten's skin filling the space between us, our fingers repeatedly brushing as we both reach for snacks.

"Would you cast a love spell on someone if you could?" he asks, elbowing me playfully.

My stomach writhes again, my skin prickling with goosebumps as my heart beats faster.

We're sitting so close together I can feel the heat of his body. His smile this close up is completely dangerous. I'm bound to do something stupid.

"Spoiler alert, but the love spell doesn't end so great for Sara," I say instead of answering.

"That wasn't what I asked." His grin widens. Is he leaning closer? No, that's ridiculous, right? I swallow hard, my eyes dropping to his lips again, full and damp and so damn inviting.

"Maybe," I say quietly.

Okay, he is *definitely* leaning in. My heart breaks into a gallop, thundering so hard I'm sure the neighbors can hear it. Is Ten going to kiss me? Why would he do that? Oh my god, Ten is going to be my first kiss. What do I do? Which way do I turn my head? What do I do with my hands?

His breath fans over my lips, but before he reaches me, my nose erupts, pouring hot, sticky blood. Fan-fucking-tastic.

"Shit." I rear back in a hurry before Ten can accidentally get a mouthful of my blood, using both hands to cover the lower part of my face, my fingers becoming instantly sticky and wet. I jump off the couch, knocking the bowl of popcorn onto the floor, and sprint for the bathroom.

I use my elbow to close the door and then use one hand to unroll a wad of toilet paper, shoving it against my nose to soak up the continued flow.

I shouldn't be surprised that my body chose to betray me at the exact moment I was about to find out what Ten's mouth feels like. Would it be entirely childish if I take a minute to rage about how unfair life is? Also, I'm clearly going to need to find somewhere new to live because that was pretty much the most humiliating moment of my entire life, and I'll obviously never be able to look him in the face again.

"Bambi?" Ten asks tentatively from the other side of the door.

If I stay quiet, will he assume I climbed out through the window and leave me alone? Or maybe I actually *should* climb out the window? Of course, then I'll be walking around the island with a blood-stained shirt, people will assume I murdered someone, things will get awkward…

I sigh. "I'm sorry. Did I get blood on you?" I ask, the words muffled through the tissues.

"I didn't catch that. Can I come in?"

I glance at myself in the mirror. My appearance is something straight out of a horror movie. I laugh, which is a horrible idea. More blood pours from my nose, soaking through the toilet paper. I toss that wad and get fresh, holding it to my nose with one hand and then the other, rinsing each in the sink so I look slightly less macabre.

"I'm fine," I say loudly, hoping that will reassure him enough that he'll go away and possibly have some sort of memory-altering event that will erase this evening from his mind entirely.

"I'd feel better if I could see for myself," he insists, his voice steady and deep. It's hard to tell with it muted through the door, but he sounds worried.

Reluctantly, I reach over and open the door. Thankfully, his white shirt appears unscathed.

"See, I'm fine," I say again, still holding toilet paper hard to my nose, waiting for the bleeding to stop. A metallic taste trickles down the back of my throat, making my stomach roil.

"Can I take a look?"

I sputter a laugh. "It's a bloody nose. What's to see?"

"I'm a doctor, remember?"

"Med student," I correct, and to my surprise, he actually looks sheepish for a second.

"I might have fudged a little. I don't know why, but it always feels less dramatic to say I left medical school than to admit I was only a few weeks from finishing my residency when I decided to change my entire life." He saunters into the bathroom, lowers the toilet lid, and sits down.

"Wow." It's hard to picture him as a doctor. To be fair, though, it's also hard to picture him as a mere mortal. "I really am okay. This happens a lot, or it used to anyway. It's one of the reasons, sadly not the *only* reason, that I'm Drew Barrymore."

He frowns again. Okay, he wasn't lying about not being a movie guy, apparently. "I've never been kissed," I clarify.

His eyebrows shoot up. "For real? *Never*? Like, *never* never?"

Fuck, this is even more embarrassing than the bloody nose. "Nope."

"Wow," he mutters this time, no doubt glad he dodged that bullet. Who wants to be a twenty-six-year-old man's first kiss? "So does that mean…?" He tugs his bottom lip between his teeth, drawing my attention to his mouth again. *Sigh*, if only my nerves had been kind enough to give me thirty seconds before ruining my life.

"What?" I ask, tossing the soaked toilet paper into the trash again and bending over to rinse my face in the sink so I can see if the bleeding has stopped.

Ten clears his throat, and I glance over while washing up, finding him doing that staring thing again. "Never mind, it's none of my business."

I tense. *Ah, of course, that's what he's wondering.* I straighten up, checking my face in the mirror. When no more blood falls, I dab myself dry with a hand towel and then lean against the sink to look at Ten again.

"I'm sure this will come as a complete shock, but I was kind of a nerd in school. Plus, I was always working or studying so I could save up for college, and then I needed to focus on my grades to keep my scholarships," I explain, ready to leave it at that, but fuck it, if I'm spilling my guts, I might as well tell him the full truth. "*Then* I took a summer job stripping to make some extra cash and something about strangers hands on me all the time just…" I shudder and shake my head. "For a while, I thought I didn't even *want* to get naked with anyone. I've gotten past that now, but you know, now I'm a twenty-six-year-old virgin, which, as it turns out, isn't as much of a turn-on as porn sells it as."

He sputters a laugh. "Well, damn."

"So you dodged a bullet. Saved by the nosebleed," I joke weakly, ignoring the knots in my stomach as his eyes meet mine again.

TEN

I wasn't *planning* on kissing Bambi, but in that moment, it felt exactly like what I wanted to be doing. Did I dodge a bullet? It doesn't feel that way. If anything, it feels like...

I shake off that half-formed thought before it can materialize. Bambi has never kissed *anyone*, and as quaint as it sounds, I feel like his first kiss should be special. I lick my lips, my whole body tingling with strange, unfamiliar feelings.

He glances down at his shirt, noticing the blood splatter there before grabbing the hem and tugging it over his head. My breath sticks in my throat as if I've never seen a shirtless man before. *Get it together, Tennyson*, I scold myself. Bambi just finished saying how much he hated being objectified when he was a stripper, which, holy shit, I can't believe he used to strip, but that's really not the point. The point is I need to stop staring.

I jump to my feet, clumsily knocking into the shelf over the toilet, causing an avalanche of toilet paper rolls and dust. Huh, I really should remember to dust more.

"Let me put on a new shirt, and we can get back to our movie marathon?" There's an edge of uncertainty in his voice like he's expecting me to tell him I'm going to leave and go to the party after all. Fat chance.

"Yeah. We're going to have to rewind, though, because I forgot to pause it, and I've gotta see what crazy shit this Nancy bitch is up to." I'm completely lost about what exactly is going on between the two of us, but I do know that I want to be right here with Bambi tonight.

He chuckles and nods before slipping out of the bathroom with his bloody T-shirt clutched in his hand. Once he's gone, I take a second to pull myself together even while my mind conjures a million confusing questions like what made me want to kiss Bambi, and was he about to kiss me back?

Before returning to the living room, I grab a couple of drinks out of the fridge and make another bag of popcorn. By the time Bambi meets me back at the couch, with a fresh shirt, I've swept up the first batch of popcorn off the floor—after having shooed the boys away from the feast they were helping themselves to in our absence—and skipped back a few scenes to where we left off.

"So, have you always loved Halloween?" I ask as soon as we're both settled. Maybe it was the unexpected revelations tonight, but I find myself curious as hell about him.

A smile immediately forms on his lips, his whole face lighting up. "My dad's birthday was on Halloween, so he would always get really into the whole season. In September, we would start having weekly horror movie marathons. We would go all out decorating the house, and every year he'd throw a huge costume party."

His expression wars between wistfulness and sadness. I don't even give it a second thought before I reach for him, grabbing his hand so he knows he's not alone, just like I did when he first told me about his dad a couple of weeks ago.

"That sounds like a lot of fun."

"It was." He uses his free hand to covertly wipe his eyes.

After that, we lapse into silence, focusing back on the movie, but he doesn't pull his hand from mine and I don't either.

Every so often, I find myself glancing at Bambi, who's endearingly enthralled in the movies I'm sure he's watched a hundred times. My heart gives a weird tug each time. What exactly is going on between the two of us? And knowing what I know now, is it right for me to even *want* anything to be going on between us?

These questions chase themselves around and around my mind through all four movies until Bambi gets to his feet with a yawn, stretching his arms over his head, his shirt riding up just enough to tempt me with another quick peek at his slim, pale stomach.

I grin to myself. Leave it to him to live in paradise and still be sorely lacking sun exposure. My fingers itch to reach out and touch him. Luckily, the rational part of my mind stops me before I can do anything stupid.

"Sleep well, Bambi."

A soft smile plays over his lips, coaxing that fluttering feeling to start in my stomach again. "You too, Ten."

CHAPTER 9

BAMBI

"Hold the fucking phone. Ten tried to kiss you?" Hen nearly knocks over his cup of tea, but Raven miraculously swoops in and snatches it up just in time. Maybe he really is psychic, or maybe he just has excellent reflexes.

"No," I say automatically, giving a sharp shake of my head. "Or, maybe...I guess?" I'm half-convinced now that I imagined the whole thing. Maybe there was something on my face Ten was going to get off for me...you know, with his mouth.

"Back up, you have to start from the beginning because you've spent weeks insisting that there's nothing between the two of you, and now *this*. I'm going to need *full* deets." He props his chin on his hands and grins at me expectantly from across the table.

"Ooh, do you want me to do a palm reading for you?" Raven offers before I can start sorting through how much to tell them about the almost kiss, or whatever it was.

"Um..."

Raven grabs a chair from the empty table next to the one Hen and I are sitting at and drags it over. "No charge," he assures me, holding his hand out expectantly.

I glance over at Hen, who shrugs as if to say, *why the hell not?* I guess it can't hurt. I give him my hand.

Raven's forehead wrinkles with concentration as he falls silent. He uses his index finger to gently trace the lines of my palm, and I try not to laugh at how much it tickles. You're probably not supposed to laugh during a psychic reading, right?

"Wow," he says after a few seconds, sending a spike of anxiety through me. Is that a good wow or a bad wow? I curl my hand closed instinctively, but Raven wraps his fingers around my wrist to keep me from jerking back. "Sorry, sweetie. You're just more of a surprise than I expected."

"What do you mean?" Holy shit, can he see that I'm a virgin just from the lines in my hand? Or maybe my short stint as a stripper? Shit, what if he can see how many times I've jerked off with my new dildo in the past couple of weeks or the sweaty dreams I have about Ten nearly every night.

Instead of answering my question, he just smiles again, his index finger tickling along my palm again as he meets my eyes. He clears his throat, and in an instant, his voice changes from his normal, airy tone to a much more dramatic, heavy one.

"You're torn between two different paths."

Hennessey snorts a laugh at the showmanship, but I sit forward, amazed that Raven called that so right. I mean, okay, it's probably true of a lot of people who come to the island, but I've never told anyone other than Ten and Nacho about the things I left behind or the fact that I'm not really sure why I'm here. And I haven't even told him about how unsure I am of what comes next.

"Does it say which is the right one to take?" I ask, looking at my hand as if the answer will be scrawled there for me to read.

"It doesn't work like that."

Of course it doesn't. I slump back in my seat, my hand still clutched in Raven's grasp.

"What *does* it say then?"

He smiles again. "I see self-discovery and that the paths you have before you won't be what you expect them to be. And, oh baby, I see love." His voice takes on a teasing, playful lilt again.

"Get it! Rawr," Hen catcalls, but my heart is beating so hard I can't give him more than a cursory smile, licking my lips and staring at my hand again.

"Really?"

"Mm-hmm." He bobs his head, still fully focused on my palm. "Heart-stopping, breath-stealing, soul mate kind of love."

"Really?" I ask breathlessly for a second time.

Hennessey makes another dismissive sound. "Just so you know, he also saw love when he did my reading. He said it would come in like a storm and then wouldn't stop cackling."

"Wait and see, Boo," Raven says, and Hen rolls his eyes.

"So, um, this soul mate..." I anxiously try to bring his attention back to my reading. I'm not sure if I believe in all this stuff or if he's just playing around, but my heart won't stop beating wildly, a silly kind of hope filling my stomach and chest.

"Be open to new experiences," he answers vaguely, finally releasing his hold on me and standing up.

"The cryptic shit is how he gets you," Hen says. "But just in case he's right, Ten is certainly a new experience."

I let out a huff of a laugh. He's not wrong about that. "You think I should, what, make a move? Tell him I want to get down and dirty?"

"I'm sure he wouldn't be opposed to either. The best thing about Ten is there's no real risk. You already know he's kind of a slut, no shade, but it's totally true. So, you can just have some casual fun with him without risking getting your heart broken."

It's Raven's turn to laugh. "Oh, honey." He shakes his head.

"It's different. I didn't *know* Easy was such a…" Hen ends his sentence by shaking his head and then focusing on me with a forced smile. "Learn from my missteps, be open from the get-go so you both know what it's all about, and you won't get your heart broken."

No risk of heartbreak, right.

I take a sip of my tea, clenching my hand into a fist. Did Raven really see anything there? I suppose it couldn't hurt to be open to new experiences anyway, just in case.

TEN

I dig through my underwear drawer, searching for my favorite pair of royal-blue briefs. I haven't worn them in a while, so they can't be in the laundry, and they aren't in the drawer, which can only mean one thing...

"Fucking cat," I mutter. God knows how he got a hold of them. How Mr. Tubbs manages any of his shenanigans is a mystery. I'm just glad underwear seems to be the only hunting trophy he's interested in because if he took one of my rats, I'd have a damn few things to say about it.

I settle for a different pair of underwear and pull them on, still not sure about my plan for the day. Bambi took off before I was up, which is something he's gotten in the habit of doing the past few days, ever since his bloody nose kiss-blocked us. I'm trying not to take his sudden absence personally, but it's not easy.

Maybe it's for the best, considering I still have no fucking earthly clue what that almost kiss meant. Should I go for it again? Bloody nose risk be damned? My stomach jolts at the thought, a combination of nerves and excitement at the thought of kissing him. But, fuck, it's complicated. *Way* more complicated than I normally like my hookups to be.

My phone buzzes on my dresser just as I'm pulling on my shorts. I pick it up to find a text from Devil asking if I'm free tonight for *dinner* at his and Angel's place. Yeah, everyone and their dad knows that dinner with Angel and Devil is never just that. What he's really inviting me over for is dessert, more specifically inviting me to *be* dessert. Hey, it works for them, and they're a damn fun time, but I can't manage a single ounce of enthusiasm for the invite. I type back a quick but polite decline and then shove my phone into my pocket and head out of the house, pausing only long enough to slip my flip-flops on.

I'm not sure where I'm headed. I just know that I need to go *somewhere* before I drive myself crazy. I wander down the street with no real direction, simply drawing in deep breaths of the salty sea air and letting it calm all of the jumbled things inside of me.

I walk by The Sand Bar and find Boston outside, power washing the front of the building.

"Hey, man, you could've given me a call to come do this."

He turns off the hose and pulls up his shirt to wipe the water droplets off his face from the mist of the spray. "I wanted to get outside and do something productive," he explains with a shrug.

"Cool." I should keep walking and let him keep working, but I find myself lingering on the sidewalk instead.

He eyes me curiously before setting the hose down and tilting his head toward the door.

"Come on, let's get a drink."

"Oh no, it's okay."

"Come on, dude, don't make me drink alone," Boston goads, and I chuckle before following him inside.

Out of habit, I immediately make my way behind the bar as he slides onto one of the stools. I mix up a couple of lemon drops, pushing one toward him and keeping one for myself. "So, what's on your mind?" I ask, bracing my hands on the weathered wood and watching him down his shot.

Boston shakes his head. "You might be behind the bar, but that's my line. What's up?"

Damn, I walked right into that one.

I pick up my shot glass and down the drink in a quick gulp and then rub my hand over my jaw as I consider his question for a few seconds. "What do you think of Bambi?"

Boston's eyebrows shoot up. "He seems like a nice kid and a good worker."

I snort. "Yeah, not exactly what I'm asking."

"I'm trying to figure out exactly what you are asking because sweet, quiet, blushing Bambi doesn't exactly seem like your type."

I want to tell him that *sweet, quiet, blushing*

Bambi has a wild side, that he was a stripper and he loves Halloween, plus he has a biting sense of humor...and a dildo, let's not forget the dildo. My throat tightens, keeping me from saying any of that. Boston's right. What am I thinking anyway? Bambi isn't the type of guy you seduce into your bed for one night of debauchery.

"You're right. Forget I said anything." I push away from the bar, my empty shot glass clutched in my hand. "He's probably not going to stay on the island forever anyway, so what's the point, right?"

"Whoa, hold on. He *might* leave eventually, and that's freaking you out? Hey, Ten, you realize tourists don't stick around either, right?" he mock-whispers as if he's letting me in on a secret.

I huff out a laugh at how ridiculous I'm being. He's right, again. The fact that Bambi won't be here forever should be an advantage if anything. There's nothing permanent to worry about, just fun.

"Fuck, I don't know. I'm all out of sorts and shit," I confess. "You should probably just ignore me."

"Did something happen between you two?"

"No." I laugh again. "I *almost* kissed him, and I'm a mess over it. What's the deal with that?"

"Wow, okay." Boston shakes his head. "I wasn't expecting that, but I guess if you're this fucked up over a kiss that didn't happen, you need to follow through and find out what it means."

I shake my head. "It's so complicated though."

"I hate to break it to you, but good relationships aren't usually the paint by numbers variety. They aren't simple because people aren't simple, and once feelings are involved, shit gets messy quickly."

My heart beats faster as my mind starts to conjure all the possibilities of what could be if I take Boston's advice and try the kiss thing again with Bambi. He might bleed all over me, or we could find out there's something real, something worth pursuing.

"You know an awful lot about relationships for a single guy who owns a bar on a gay resort island," I tease.

He snorts and nudges his shot glass toward me for a refill. "Yeah, fair warning, you might not want to listen to a damn thing I say, considering I've never managed to make a relationship work. But I *have* had a fair few near misses in my life, and those are the ones I still think about, still wonder what could have been."

I refill both glasses and pass his back to him while I consider his advice. "To finding out what could have been before it's too late," I finally say, holding my glass out toward him.

"Here, here." Boston clinks his glass to mine, and we both down our shots.

CHAPTER 10

BAMBI

I've never heard a rat snore, but it's genuinely the cutest thing I've ever experienced in my life to have Fred and Barney both curled up together on my chest, taking a midday nap after having spent the morning begging me for treats and scurrying around the living room. As for me, I'm still in my pajamas, trying to convince myself to do something other than watch TV and play with the rats today.

Of course, at some point, Ten will come home from wherever he is, and I'm sure that'll be all the motivation I need to get off my ass and leave the house so I look like less of a shut-in. Also, I'm still working through the epic humiliation of him knowing I'm a virgin with overactive nasal blood vessels.

As if summoned by my thoughts, the sound of the front door opening meets my ears. My whole body tenses, but with the rats still sleeping soundly—aw, oh my god, Barney's little foot is twitching while he dreams—I can't jump up and bolt down the hallway to my bedroom like I want to. Shit, fuck. I wonder if there's any possibility at all that Ten is like a T-rex, and he won't see me if I stay *very* still.

His footsteps grow louder, and within a few seconds, he steps into the living room. A smile spreads over his face when he sees me, the staying-still plan epically failing. His hair is wet, his skin almost glowing with how golden it is from the sun.

"Hey, Bambi. I was starting to wonder if you'd moved out without telling me," he jokes, but there's a momentary tightening of his expression that fills me with guilt.

"It turns out having friends is really time-consuming." That part isn't a lie. Hanging out with Hen is fun, but it's also been a lot.

He laughs, and then his eyes move over me, taking me in entirely. I'm bracing for a joke about the fact that I'm still in my pajamas or maybe questions about if I'm planning to do anything other than sit around and play with the rats all day.

"Have you been to the waterfall?" Ten asks instead, surprising me.

"No." I don't tack on that I haven't ventured away from the main part of town much.

His smile returns in full force, his eyes

dancing with infectious mischievous excitement. "Want to go on an adventure?"

My heart rate kicks up. Raven said to be open to new experiences, and while I doubt he meant hiking, this might be a good first step.

"Okay." I grin back and then look down at the rats still sleeping soundly on me. "But what about them?"

Ten crosses the room and rattles the treat box near their cage. Their eyes pop open instantly, little noses twitching. Barney yawns while Fred hurries to get his chubby little butt over to where the treats are as fast as he can.

Once both boys are back in their house, I dip into my bedroom to get dressed. I don't have the first clue what a person wears to go hiking, so I wing it, putting on a pair of shorts and a plain T-shirt and then digging my tennis shoes out.

When I return to the living room, Ten is dressed similarly, leaning on the couch and waiting for me. This time when he looks me up and down, I swear the air crackles between us like it's electrified. That has to be my imagination, doesn't it? Sure, there was that strange, unexplainable almost kiss, but there's no way he's actually *interested* in me.

I awkwardly shove my hands into my pockets and then pull them back out, licking my dry lips. I swear Ten's eyes track the movement of my tongue. My body heats as this charged moment drags on and on until Ten finally breaks it by pushing off the couch.

"Come on, let's go see the waterfall."

I nod, dragging in a deep breath to steady myself, and then follow him out of the house.

"Where were you this morning?" I ask as we walk down the street in the direction of the mountains.

"Surfing," he answers. "The waves were incredible." The reverence in his voice draws me in. "It's like the ultimate feeling of freedom. There's so much clarity out there on the ocean. It's better than therapy." He looks over at me, and I get caught in his gaze for a few seconds.

"It sounds amazing," I manage to say. "Maybe you could teach me." Did I really just suggest that?

He groans as if I asked him for something much filthier than a surfing lesson. "Oh, baby, you will not regret putting me in charge of your surfing cherry."

I sputter a laugh, and he throws an arm around me, leaning in until his lips brush my ear. "I promise, I'll be gentle."

My stomach flutters violently and my breath hitches. "Okay."

TEN

"I'm sorry, I must've taken a wrong turn somewhere," I apologize as we fight our way through the drastically overgrown path that I'm almost positive won't lead us to the waterfall. I frown, going back over the route we took in my mind. I could've sworn this was the right way, but nothing looks correct now.

"I thought you hiked up here a lot." It's obvious Bambi is *trying* to keep the accusation out of his tone but failing miserably.

"I do. That's why I can't figure out where I went wrong. We took the East path, the fork toward the left, and then kept straight. The waterfall should've smacked us in the face at least a mile back."

Bambi puffs out heavy breaths behind me, trudging noisily through the weeds and low-hanging branches.

"Awesome. We're lost, and we're going to die out here. This is why I prefer to sit at home watching movies."

I bite back a laugh. "We're not going to die. I know the exact directions we took to get here, so it will be easy to get back. What I can't figure out is who moved the damn waterfall."

"Must've been Harold," Bambi jokes. "Does that fall under typical ghostly powers?"

I snort. "I have no fucking clue. Oh hey, it looks like there's a clearing up here. We can at least sit down and catch our breath for a little bit before turning around."

"Thank you, thank you, thank you."

I can't believe I fucked this up so badly. I've been to the waterfall plenty of times. It's not that difficult to find. I had a whole plan. We'd dip our feet into the water and enjoy the beauty of nature, and then I'd make another attempt to kiss him. It seemed like an appropriately memorable first kiss for him, the perfect romantic atmosphere. I thought old Harry was supposed to *help* with this romance shit, not get us lost in the woods.

The trees start to thin, and we crash into the clearing. A laugh forces its way out of my throat as I take in the field full of violet ironweed wildflowers and the faded old carousel Harold built for his partner.

"Is that the rainbow carousel?" Bambi asks, coming to a stop beside me.

"It must be. I've never been here." I've hiked nearly every inch of these woods, but I've never had much interest in going out of my way to find the carousel.

The legend says that this was the last thing Harold built on the island as an anniversary gift for the love of his life, George. It became their favorite place on the island, and they even visited it the day before they passed away. Everyone says his spirit is heavy throughout the island but nowhere as strong as here.

"People say it only works if Harold approves of a love match," Bambi says with obvious amusement, no longer seeming overly tired as he crosses the field toward the carousel.

"Do you believe in that stuff?" I ask, following him, picking a few flowers along the way while butterflies and honeybees flutter and buzz around me.

"What? That there's a romance-obsessed ghost actually haunting the island? Or do I believe in soul mates in general?" he asks, stopping in front of the control panel to study the buttons.

"Both. Either." I pluck a long strand of grass and use it to tie a messy bouquet together.

"Not really." He shrugs and starts pressing the dirt-crusted buttons. "I think when we die, we're gone. And I think love is way too complicated to rest on two people being *destined* for each other." The carousel stays stubbornly stationary. "And I think a carousel out in the woods with zero maintenance is bound to be finicky."

"Yeah." He makes some good points, and I've never believed in the ghost thing per se, but... "It's kind of a nice thought, though, isn't it?"

"What's that?" He climbs onto the carousel anyway, running his hands across the multicolored horses. The golden poles that connect them to the ride are flaky and rusty. The rainbow colors that were once vibrant are all muted and dull. He's right. This poor thing gets no maintenance. Someone should start taking care of it, maybe give it a good paint job.

"I don't know, the idea that Harold and George are still together somewhere and that they care about the love lives of everyone who sets foot on the island." I feel a little silly even saying it aloud. I've never considered myself to be any kind of romantic, mostly opting for casual, simple encounters over the hard work of building and maintaining a real relationship, but maybe there's a part of me just waiting for someone who feels worth all that effort.

I climb onto the carousel too, and Bambi turns to look at me, his eyes landing on the bouquet of wildflowers clutched in my hand. I thrust it toward him awkwardly, every ounce of charm and every play in my book suddenly gone, leaving me feeling like a fumbling idiot with my first real crush.

Bambi's cheeks turn that sweet shade of pink I love, his eyes going wide as he reaches for the flowers with a trembling hand. "Thank you."

I wrap my hand around the cool metal pole and lean in slowly, giving him every opportunity to push me away or tell me to stop. He doesn't do either. Bambi's eyelids flutter closed, the moment stretching out endlessly between us as if time itself is holding its breath.

And then our lips meet. I've lost track of how many men I've kissed in my life, from my very first behind the garage at a party in tenth grade to the blur of tourists and locals alike since I came to the island and dozens in between. Somewhere in all of that, I started to think kissing was highly overrated, nothing but a prelude to the main event, a courtesy to be checked off before *getting off*.

Fuck was I wrong.

Bambi gasps against my mouth, the bouquet of flowers tumbling out of his hand and landing at our feet as I wrap my arms around him and pull him closer. His lips part, and I deepen the kiss, sweeping my tongue into his mouth to taste him, the sweet flavor of his tongue stroking my cock to life and sending electricity cascading down my spine. His lips are a little clumsy under mine, stumbling after the kiss eagerly while I sink into it, coaxing him to open for me so I can taste more of him.

Without warning, the carousel lurches, throwing our balance off and sending us toppling into each other with a fit of laughter.

"I think that means Harold approves," I joke, catching my balance against the nearest horse and holding on to Bambi again so he doesn't fall.

"Or it means that one of those buttons I pushed actually worked. It just took a minute since the wiring on this thing is old and shitty."

I lean in, brushing my lips over his earlobe, adding the way he shivers against me to the list of ways he's adorably addictive. "It never hurts to believe in a little magic," I whisper before nipping at his ear, eliciting another fit of laughter from him as he leans into me, our bodies fitting together perfectly.

His hand finds its way to my chest. Can he feel the way my heart is beating completely out of control?

"Can we stay here and enjoy the ride for a little while?" he asks. I nod, only realizing he's referring to the carousel when he slips out of my grasp and climbs onto a large, white horse that's tossing its head wildly, its mane the same faded rainbow as the roof of the ride.

I grin at him, picking the flowers back up

and then clambering onto the horse beside his.

I'm totally down for enjoying the ride.

CHAPTER 11

BAMBI

My heart is *still* pounding by the time we make it back to town, and not because I'm woefully out of shape for hiking. Ten *kissed* me. His lips were on *my* lips. His freaking tongue was *in my mouth*.

I sneak a glance at him out of the corner of my eye and clutch the bouquet tighter in my hand. I spent the entire hike back trying to work up the courage to ask what any of this means. Ten probably kisses lots of people, right? I really shouldn't read into it. I should be happy to be one of the many, and I am. I finally got my first kiss, it was with Ten, *and* I didn't even get a nosebleed this time.

I bring the wildflowers to my nose and inhale the muted scent. Would it be too sentimental to press them to save? After all, this day is well worth remembering. I find my steps slowing as we walk down the main street, getting closer and closer to home, nowhere near ready for today to end.

We stayed and enjoyed the carousel so long that the sun is starting to set now, casting the buildings in a dusky light, the air beginning to chill from the warmth of the day.

"It's always weird for me to see the bar empty like this," I muse as it comes into view.

"No one dancing in the street or making out up against the building," Ten says with amusement, slowing his steps as well. Our hands have been bumping while we walked, but he reaches for my hand now, threading his fingers through mine and dragging me toward the bar. "Come on."

"What are we doing?" I ask as he leads me over to the front door and tests to see if it's locked. Nothing on the island ever is, so of course, the door swings open easily, revealing the quiet, dark bar inside. "Are we allowed to do this?" I whisper this time as if Boston will pop out of the darkness and scold us for trespassing when The Sand Bar is closed.

"What's Boston going to do? Call the cops on us?" Ten laughs at the absurdity of the idea.

He reaches over with his free hand to flick on the lights, and we let the door swing closed behind us. "Is it weird that it looks *smaller* empty like this?"

I set my flowers down on one of the tables

and walk over to the empty space where people usually dance—and by dance, I mean basically fuck in public to the rhythm of the music. Ten makes his way around the bar, and I stop to watch him, a familiar feeling washing over me. How many nights did I spend sneaking looks at him, conjuring fantasies that he might look up and notice me one day?

Now he has, and I don't have the first clue what comes next. It's terrifying and thrilling all at once.

He starts mixing a drink, looking up at me with a smirk when he's finished, setting a glass full of the red and orange concoction on the bar. "Sorry, no fresh cherries at the moment."

"Is that a Sex on the Beach?" I ask, walking over to pick it up, remembering the very first day I wandered in here, completely lost, in more ways than one.

I'd set eyes on the hottest bartender I'd ever seen in my life and became completely tongue-tied. He asked what he could get me, and I instantly forgot what drinks even were, let alone the names of any. After a few seconds of awkwardly staring at him, he mixed me up a drink that looked exactly like this and pushed it across the bar toward me. *Sex on the Beach fixes all of life's problems,* he'd told me with a wink.

"Was I right? Did it solve all of your problems the first time?" He makes a second one for himself and leans forward on the bar, studying me with eyes that feel like they're seeing too much and not enough all at once.

"It solved a few of them," I admit with a laugh, wrapping my lips around the straw and taking a sip.

He holds my gaze for several heartbeats, the air in the room seeming to stand still around us. It's on the tip of my tongue to ask him what exactly is happening between us, but I can't make myself ask and ruin it. If the answer is he's just curious about me or has always had a fantasy of deflowering someone…well, maybe it's better to just let things happen and not worry about the why of it all.

Ten reaches under the bar for something, and a few seconds later, the jukebox comes to life, lighting up and playing "This is Love" by Bob Marley. He gasps dramatically. "I think Harry wants us to dance."

I roll my eyes, my smile widening as a too-big feeling fills my chest. "Right, you definitely don't have a remote back there."

He scoffs. "You're insulting Harold now. I think you're going to need to repent before he curses you."

"Do I now?" I raise both eyebrows at him,

and he nods sagely before coming around the bar and offering me his hand.

"I think a dance should appease him."

A giggle slips from my lips, and I take his hand, letting him lead me back over to the open space on the floor. Yet another thing I've never done, dancing with someone. Luckily, Ten seems to have some idea what he's doing, tugging me against him and wrapping one arm around my middle while keeping our hands clasped.

He's a good few inches taller than me, his body hard from all of the time he spends doing physical activities and yoga. He smells like the ocean and sunshine, and my heart is beating so hard I'm sure he can feel it with our bodies pressed so close together like this. I follow his lead, swaying to the music while he croons along with the song, his voice rich and mesmerizing.

Can I bottle this moment and save it forever?

Before I can give myself a chance to overthink anything, my lips are on Ten's again. His mouth is warm on mine, giving way to the kiss eagerly. Every inch of my body heats instantly, electricity buzzing over my skin, my knees trembling so badly I can barely hold myself up. Luckily, Ten has me.

The kiss on the carousel was sweet. Even

when our tongues got involved, it felt surprisingly chaste. This time, the fire between us seems to spill over. I don't have the first clue what I'm doing as I grapple with his clothes, our tongues sliding over each other as Ten backs me up until I bump into one of the tables.

I pant into his mouth as the hard outline of his arousal presses against me, making my stomach squirm with nerves even while my cock throbs against him. Every inch of me quakes with anxious excitement. Is he going to fuck me right here? Am I even ready for that? He grabs my ass and kisses me deeper.

I twist my hands around the front of his shirt, gasping when he drags his mouth off mine and starts to kiss down my throat. I let my head fall back, an embarrassingly loud moan slipping out of my mouth when he nibbles on my Adam's apple and grinds his cock on me through our clothes.

And then a throat clears behind us...

TEN

With my tongue down Bambi's throat, my hands on his ass, his body plastered against mine, I'm pretty sure a herd of buffalo could run through the bar, and I wouldn't notice. Case in point, it's only when Bambi pushes my chest that

I realize we aren't alone.

I look up to find Boston standing a few feet away, his arms crossed over his broad chest, an eyebrow arched in amusement. I offer him a sheepish smile.

"Hey, man. How'd you know we were here?"

"Silent alarm," he answers gruffly.

"Oh shit, really?"

He snorts a laugh, relaxing his stance. "No, dumbass, I walked by and saw the lights on."

"That makes a hell of a lot more sense." I run my hands through my short hair and glance at Bambi, who's all flushed and anxious, sort of half-ducked behind the chair that's up on the table as if he's hoping Boston won't actually see him. "Do you need us to get out of here?"

"Nah, just don't drink *all* my booze, and if you fuck, clean up after yourselves. I don't want to find crusted cum on the tables or floor later."

Bambi makes a strangled noise, making me wonder if someone can actually die of embarrassment and whether I'm going to need to know how to perform CPR.

I give Boston a lazy salute. "You got it."

He shakes his head at us and then turns to walk back out, taking the heated mood from just moments before with him.

Maybe it's not the worst thing though. Bambi straightens his clothing and fidgets anxiously. I'm used to zero to sixty. I'm used to guys who are just as eager to hit it and quit it as I am. This is completely different, and it's occurring to me possibly later than it should have that I don't have the first fucking clue what I'm doing with a guy like Bambi. All this cheesy romance stuff, am I getting it right? This is all new for him, so he probably wants to take things slowly, but what does that even look like?

I'm so in over my head.

"Should we finish our drinks?" he asks when I've gone entirely too long without saying anything.

I clear my throat and try to ignore the way my heart is racing for completely different reasons now. "Yeah."

We make our way back over to the bar while I let the jukebox cycle through the island music, low in the background now.

I pull two stools down, and we sit with our drinks, the atmosphere between us heavy with uncertainty.

"Fuck, I wish I knew how to do this," I confess before taking a sip of my drink.

He twirls his straw between his teeth,

studying me for a few seconds and then laughing. "If you don't even know how to do this, we're in trouble because you have a hell of a lot more experience than I do."

"Not at dating. Sex, I know how to do, but *this*?" I gesture between us. "Yeah, I'm lost."

His eyes widen a fraction. "Dating? Is that what this is, a date?" he asks, setting his drink down and absently using his thumb to gather beads of condensation off the glass.

I bounce my knee, fighting the urge to laugh at how ridiculous the nerves bubbling inside of me are. I'm thirty-six years old, shouldn't I be better at this? I guess this is the price to pay for skipping all the feelings shit before. Now I don't have the first clue how to go about it.

"I don't know," I admit. "Just for fun, let's try it out tonight to see how it feels."

"Okay, so you want to make first-date small talk or something?" he asks, eyeing me skeptically.

"Sure, why not? Let's see, we already talked family and hobbies. We know about each other's jobs and friends." I drum my fingers on the bar while I think. "Oh, I've got it, something about you no one knows."

"You already know something no one else knows," he reminds me.

"I guess that means I need to even the score. Okay, here it goes." I lean forward, and Bambi automatically does the same, almost as if it's involuntary. His hair is a bit tousled from our kissing, his lips pink and puffy, and how do those big blue eyes of his just keep getting bigger? "I'm afraid of pugs."

He stares at me for a second and then starts to laugh. "What? Come on. You mean the little flat-faced, chubby dogs?"

"Have you ever heard how they bark? They sound like terrifying little demons," I defend.

"I don't think I've even met a pug that has all of its teeth. Oh my god, I saw one once that had a tongue that was too big for its mouth, so it was always walking around with it hanging out like a total dope."

He falls into another fit of laughter.

"Hey, I didn't laugh at your secret," I feign outrage.

"You should. It's ridiculous," he says when he composes himself. "Who's a virgin in their late twenties?"

Without thinking, I reach over and put my hand on his thigh. Bambi drops his eyes to look at it but doesn't flinch back or push me away. If anything, he seems to lean into the touch.

"I'm sure there are plenty of people. And it's actually really cool that you saved all your firsts instead of just hopping into bed with guys you didn't even like to get it over with."

"Do people really do that?"

I shrug. "I'm sure some do."

"Have you liked all the guys you've had sex with?" he asks, wrapping his lips around his straw again and sucking down the rest of his drink. My eyes linger for several seconds on the shape his lips make and the way his throat bobs as he swallows, my cock thickening again.

He looks at me expectantly. Oh, right, he asked me a question.

"Honestly, I hardly even knew most of the guys I've had sex with." I don't have an ounce of shame about my sex life, but as I watch Bambi sway in his seat to the music, every inch of him looking kissable as fuck, radiating all the sweetness that I can't get enough of, I think I want to try it a different way this time.

The question is, am I going to be able to figure out how?

CHAPTER 12

TEN

"Whoop!" Trick's exuberant shout is nearly lost in the sound of the ocean and the wind. The sky is getting darker by the minute. A storm brewing over the Atlantic is quickly making its way to the island, creating perfect conditions for an hour or so of kite surfing.

I tighten my grip on my rope as another strong gust comes through, catching my kite and pulling me a good ten feet into the air, my stomach swooping and my heart soaring with the adrenaline of my brief moment airborne before I meet the water again. Cool droplets cling to my face from the ocean spray, but I can't spare a hand to wipe them off, so I do the best I can by shaking my head like a wet dog, smiling like a fool the whole time.

When the rain actually starts to fall around us, we guide ourselves back to shore, gather up our shit, and make a run for the gazebo that's just down the beach to wait out the initial downpour.

"Shit." Easy laughs as we reach the shelter, ditching our stuff in the wet sand outside of it and then crowding in.

"It was bound to happen," Lux says, his voice full of as much amusement as everyone else's.

"Is there any other way to live than this?" Trick asks with a content sigh as we all watch the dark clouds overhead dump their heavy burden over the ocean.

"If there is, I don't want to know about it." I shake my head and then use both hands to get the water off my face.

There's a wild kind of beauty in watching a storm over the ocean. It's destructive and restorative all at once. I'm struck suddenly with the feeling that I wish Bambi were out here with me to see this.

After we got home last night, I felt even more unsteady and unsure of how to act. If he were anyone else, I would've pulled him into my bedroom and done filthy things to him. The way he lingered in the hallway outside of my door, the two of us staring at each other for a few seconds, I started to wonder if that's what he wanted me to do. But then he kissed my cheek, said goodnight, and disappeared into his room.

He was still asleep when I ran out the door

this morning to meet the guys before we missed our window to kitesurf.

"How do you take things slow?" I blurt, all three of my friends turning to look at me with various confused expressions. "In a relationship or whatever," I clarify. None of their stupefied expressions ease. "Never mind, what am I asking you bunch of sluts for?"

Easy snorts. "Yeah, *slow* isn't exactly in my vocabulary. You're going to have to tell us all about locking down Bambi now though." He waggles his eyebrows.

"What?" I sputter. "I haven't locked anyone down."

"Uh-huh." He gives me a maddening, knowing smirk.

"My version of wooing a man is just driving him so fucking batshit he wants to murder me, so I'm probably not going to be much help." Trick shrugs.

"I'm pretty sure I've forgotten what sex even is," Lux says unhelpfully.

"I need different friends," I complain, and they all laugh.

"Oh, hey, look, help has arrived." Trick nods, and I turn to see what he's talking about.

Hennessey comes running down the

beach, his hands helplessly over his head to block some of the rain. He barrels into our shelter without hesitation, sparing a brief glare at Easy. Clearly, the need to get out of the rain is stronger than his desire to avoid Easy.

"Perfect timing. You can help Ten out here with his relationship questions," Trick says, clapping me on the back and grinning at Hen.

A harsh laugh bursts from his lips. "Yeah, clearly I'm a relationship genius."

"Is everyone on this island either a slut or a dumbass?" I ask, and they all exchange looks.

Trick shrugs. "Yeah, I think so."

"So, I'm on my own trying to figure out how to do this thing with Bambi?" I sigh.

"You and Bambi?" Hen stops in the middle of ringing out his T-shirt and perks up. "Details, please."

"There's nothing to tell." Even if there was, I'm not about to go blurting all of our business to these vultures. Holy shit, that's different. I've never had a problem telling the guys about my sexcapades before, but with Bambi, it just feels wrong.

"He's sweet," Hen says, an edge of defensiveness in his voice.

"I know."

"And if you hurt him, I'm going to cut off your balls and feed them to you." He fixes me with a look so deadly, I'm pretty sure he would actually do it.

I hold up my hands in surrender. "Damn, okay, got it."

"I don't have any spectacular advice, but I think your best bet is to be honest with him and listen to him," Easy says, surprising all of us based on everyone's shocked expressions.

"Like a proper adult?" I ask skeptically.

"It's worth a shot. And, hey, if that doesn't work, eat his ass like you're in a pie-eating contest."

Now that's the Easy I'm used to. We all laugh.

Eventually, the rain lets up to a gentle drizzle. Hen bids us all goodbye, giving Easy the finger, and then takes off. The rest of us gather up our stuff and head back down the beach.

"Want to surf a little longer?" Easy asks.

"Nah, I'm going to head home."

"Give Bambi a big kiss from all of us," Easy teases, and I follow Hen's example and give him the finger.

I bungee my kitesurfing gear to the roof of

my golf cart and head for home with a smile I can't wipe off my face.

BAMBI

No note, no coffee, no sign of Ten. Yup, he totally regrets yesterday's kiss. Well, *kisses*. Who can blame him? I was probably horrible at it. I anxiously scrub a non-existent spot on the counter.

It'll be fine. When he gets home, I'll be totally nonchalant. Eventually, things won't be awkward. It'll be fine.

My lips tingle with the memory of Ten's mouth on mine last night. I stood in the hallway for at least a solid minute, the two of us staring at each other while I tried to work up the nerve to make a move. That was probably my one and only chance with him, and I couldn't summon the guts to do more than kiss him. This is why I'm still a virgin. Ugh.

The door opens right behind me, making my heart leap into my throat as I spin around to see Ten stepping inside. He's drenched, his hair so wet that droplets of water are trickling down his face. He's nearly naked, the only scrap of clothing on his body a skimpy black Speedo that's barely containing the bulge of his cock.

My breath catches and my skin heats.

"My wetsuit was soaked," he explains, pointing somewhere behind him, possibly to indicate that he took it off and hung it up outside. I have no idea because I can't tear my eyes off his body. "Wow, I'm feeling so objectified."

My face heats and I slam my hands over my eyes because that's really the only way I'm going to stop staring at him. "I'm sorry."

His laughter is deep and warm, like the crackle of a fire. "I'm fucking with you, Bambi. Look all you want."

I shake my head rapidly. That would *not* be a good idea. "I promise, I won't keep staring at you and making things weird. In fact, if you want me to move out or off the island, I totally understand. I know the kiss was just a one-time thing, don't worry, I'm not going to turn into a stage-five clinger or anything."

My hands are still over my eyes, so I have no idea what Ten's reaction is, but I feel good that I got that all out there right away so he won't have to feel awkward around me. I hear his footsteps on the linoleum kitchen floor, and a moment later, his cool, damp fingers are wrapping around my wrists, pulling my hands away from my eyes.

Did he get taller since last night? Or maybe it's just how close he's standing. I tilt my head to look at his face, hovering only a few inches from mine, the salty scent of the ocean radiating off him, adding to the very distinct impression that he's some kind of sea god come to life.

"Are you saying all that because you don't want to kiss me again or because you think I don't want to kiss you?"

"You left so early, and you didn't even leave a note or coffee like you normally do," I reason.

"I wanted to get to the beach before I missed the good wind. I'll make you coffee right now if it helps." His lips quirk in a mesmerizing half-smile.

"So you weren't avoiding me while trying to figure out how to let me down easily?"

He huffs out a laugh. "There really are a lot of dumbasses on this island."

"Wha—"

Ten cuts my question off with a firm, full press of his lips on mine. He tastes salty this morning, no doubt from the ocean. It should be gross, but it's Ten, and the sea is part of him. It mixes perfectly with his natural scents and flavors, making me all the more desperate for him.

My heart hammers wildly. Does this mean he wants more? I didn't mess this up or miss my chance by chickening out last night? I wrap my arms around his neck and press my mouth even harder to his, starting to get the hang of this kissing thing. I follow the rhythm of his lips with my own, the open and close of our mouths like waves of their own.

He breaks the kiss and rests his forehead on mine. "I still have no fucking clue what I'm doing, but I can promise you I won't pull any bullshit games."

I nod, bumping our noses together.

I'm afraid to ask what exactly this all means, but that promise makes me feel a little sturdier on my feet.

"Okay," I murmur.

"It's supposed to be shitty and rainy the rest of the day. What do you say to a movie marathon?" he suggests, and I smile even wider.

"You're on."

CHAPTER 13

TEN

I groan at the twinge in my back as the muscles tense painfully. I grit my teeth, trying to convince myself that it's not so bad, that a few ibuprofen and morning yoga will have me in good enough shape for the wakeboarding we have planned today. There have been too many good storms lately, which means too much kite surfing, which is absolute hell on my muscles.

There are major benefits to Lux owning the island's boat and sport equipment rental. During the off-season, he lets us use whatever we want. I make a move to get off the couch and gasp when my muscles constrict again, tightening around my spine.

"Fuck," I mutter, gritting my teeth as I pull my phone out of my pocket. I pull up the group text and type out a new message.

TEN: Sorry, guys, can't make it this morning. My back is fucked.

TRICK: Boo. Too much wild sex with Bambi throw your back out?

I shake my head and grin. Nope, no wild sex with Bambi...*yet*. But for a change, that doesn't feel like the end-all. In fact, spending the day watching movies with him a couple of days ago, making out like teenagers and talking about our lives before we moved to the island, was the most perfect day I've had in ages.

TEN: Nope

EASY: Fuck, that sucks. Want me to swing by Lyric's and get some edibles for you? Your back will still hurt, but you won't give a fuck.

TEN: Thanks, but I think I just need to take it easy for a few days, maybe sweet talk Devil into letting me use the hot tub at one of his rentals.

LUX: At the risk of sounding like these two bozos, get Bambi to give you a massage;)

TEN: Ha, yeah, maybe. You guys have fun. I'll hit you up in a couple of days when I'm able to move my ass off the couch again.

I get a flurry of thumbs-up messages in return.

I lazily toss my phone onto the couch beside me and let my head fall back. I usually dread these flare-ups, leaving me trapped in the house for days on end, bored out of my fucking mind. But when I hear Bambi's bedroom door open down the hall, I find myself smiling.

Maybe it won't be so bad to be laid up for a day or two if I'm not here all alone. His footsteps draw closer until he appears in the entrance to the living room, all sleep rumpled and adorable. His blond hair sticks up in all directions, lines from his pillow are etched on his cheek. He looks at me and his eyes get a little wider, the slightest blush creeping up his neck and over his cheeks.

Fuck, I like the way he looks at me. My stomach flutters, and for a few seconds, I forget about the pain in my back or the fact that I still very much have no damn clue what I'm doing, and I just smile back at him.

"Morning," he murmurs and then yawns.

"Morning," I say back, patting the cushion next to me. He takes the hint, crossing the room. He sits down, angling his body toward me, one leg tucked up, and one arm hooked over the back of the couch.

The move is so much more casual than it was even a few days ago, familiar even. My body heats and my cock swells, tenting my shorts. No man has ever affected me this way, and I haven't even seen him naked yet. Is it possible that's *why* he's burrowing so far under my skin? He feels like a mystery. Like he's unattainable even sitting six inches away from me.

"Why are you looking at me like that?" he asks, and I give in to the urge to reach for him, brushing my fingers over his thigh, just where his sleep shorts are riding up. Goosebumps rise along his skin, his dark leg hair standing on end as he shivers and leans into my touch.

"How am I looking at you?" I ask with a smirk.

"What?" Bambi's breathless, the color in his cheeks darker now, his lips parted with each heavy breath.

My cock likes that *way too much*. Dammit, I really am bad at taking it slow.

I chuckle and drag my fingers just a little higher, watching his cock stiffen and press against the front of his shorts too. It's obvious he's not wearing any underwear underneath them, the outline of his cock mouthwatering and perfect.

Fuck, I need to get a hold of myself before I push him too far or make him uncomfortable. I pull my hand back, and the fog in his eyes clears, almost as if losing my touch breaks whatever spell he was under. He blinks a few times and then smiles, jumping to his feet.

"Coffee," he says in a raspy voice.

"Oh shit, sorry, I haven't made any yet. I was working up to getting off the couch to get that bottle of ibuprofen over there." I point across the room. "Coffee was the next feat on my list after that."

That's all it takes for any hint of shy lust to be cleared from his expression entirely. "What's wrong? Are you hurt?" Bambi rakes his eyes over me, full of concern that warms me almost as much as the *fuck-me* look did.

"It's just my back. Remember when I mentioned the car accident that ultimately brought me here? Well, I have all these pins in my back, and sometimes when I go too hard, or when my body just wants to fuck with me, my back seizes up for a couple of days. I'll be fine. I just need to take it easy."

He frowns. "I'm going to take care of you." He looks so serious, a little furrow between his brow. With the way he straightens his shoulders as if he's declaring his intentions to take on some epic task, I can't help but laugh.

I find myself reaching for him again, sliding my fingers between his and giving his hand a squeeze. "You're sweet, Bambi. You don't need to worry about me."

He tsks, squeezing my fingers back before dropping my hand and crossing the room to get the bottle of NSAIDs. He pours a few into his hand and then offers them to me.

"Stay right here. I can make coffee. What do you want for breakfast? Eggs? Oh, I could make French toast. Do we have bread?"

My smile gets even bigger, and my heart does this fluttery thing, my stomach swooping like I just caught a major wave.

"There's bread in the freezer. I keep it there so it doesn't go bad too quickly. You can use it for French toast."

"Perfect." He turns to leave the room.

"Bambi," I call after him, and he pauses in the doorway. "Thank you."

He shoots me a sweet smile over his shoulder. "Don't mention it."

BAMBI

I probably shouldn't have been quite so confident about the way I casually declared that I could make French toast. Stitch up a wound, sure, I've practiced that. Make French toast? Not so much. But it's fine. I can figure it out. How hard could it really be?

It occurs to me that Nacho left the island to study at a patisserie in France. He must know how to make French toast, right? I grope for my phone in my pocket and call him.

"Hello?" he answers on the third ring, his voice sounding raspy and confused.

"I'm sorry. I didn't mean to wake you."

"Qui C'est?" another muffled voice asks. Double shit, he's not alone, and now I'm *really* making a pest of myself.

"Shh, go back to sleep. Hold on a second, sweetie." I hear distant sounds and then the click of a door being pulled closed. "Is everything okay?" Nacho asks.

"Yeah, everything's great." A warm glow starts in my chest and radiates through me as I think about the way Ten was looking at me, the way he was *touching* me just a few minutes ago. "Sorry, I thought it would be later in the day where you are."

He chuckles. "It is. I just haven't quite made it out of bed yet."

"Right, sorry."

"Don't worry about it. What's up?"

"I was calling to ask how to make French toast."

His laugh on the other end of the phone is just as raspy as his voice is this morning. "Have you ever heard of Google?" he teases.

I wedge the phone between my ear and shoulder to free up my hands, so I can start the coffee while talking to him. Of course I've heard of Google. Maybe this was just an excuse to call my friend, who I've been horrible at staying in touch with since he left weeks ago.

"Yes, but if I Google it, how can I be sure it's the *best* recipe. I don't want to serve Ten terrible French toast."

Nacho gasps and then makes a muffled squealing sound. Oh crap. I cringe, realizing my mistake a little too late.

"You and Ten? Tell me everything. How did it happen? How many times has he fucked you? Or are you the top? I could totally see you shedding that whole shy, innocent thing for some *major* top energy."

I sputter and nearly fumble my phone. "Nacho," I mutter his name and bury my face in my hands even though he can't see me right now. "We haven't..."

"Damn." He sighs. "Really? Nothing?"

"Well, not *nothing*." I pour the coffee grounds into the filter basket and lean against the counter. "We kissed...a few times now, actually."

Nacho makes another excited sound. "So, wait, is this like a *thing*? You're kissing but not fucking. You're making him French toast. Is my baby boy falling in *love*?"

"No," I say firmly, forcing a laugh as my heart attempts to beat its way out of my chest. Ten isn't falling in love with me. Of course he's not. "I'm still not even sure that I'm staying." I'm not sure who I'm trying to convince, him or me. "It's temporary, and it's fun, that's all."

"Okay." He doesn't sound convinced. "Tell you what, I'll text you a recipe really quick, but you have to promise to call and fill me in on everything later, got it?"

"Yeah," I agree. "I promise."

"Perfect. Now, I have to get back to bed. There is a dick just *begging* for a morning blowjob in there."

I chuckle. "And a person attached to it, I'm assuming?"

"Sure, of course," he agrees dismissively. "Love you, boo, talk to you later."

We hang up, and a couple of minutes later, my phone vibrates with a typed-out recipe and instructions for making French toast.

It's actually pretty easy, and in no time at

all, I'm carrying a plate and mug of coffee into the living room for Ten.

"You are a godsend," he says, his praise making me feel all kinds of giddy.

I go back to grab my breakfast and then settle onto the couch next to him. "I had to call Nacho to ask how to make this," I confess.

"You don't cook much?"

"No. My dad *loved* to cook, so he did it all when I was growing up. While I was in college, I worked to pay for a meal plan, and then when I got here, Nacho loved to cook too. I guess I've never had much of a chance."

"My mom is a *terrible* cook," he says, a fond smile and a faraway look coming over his face. "So, I cooked a lot when I lived at home, and I realized I really like it."

"Are you close?" It occurs to me that while we talked about a lot of things the other night —in between learning the topography of each other's mouths with our tongues—family didn't come up. Maybe he didn't want to ruin the mood by bringing up my dad again?

"Oh yeah. My parents are great. They hate that I live all the way out here, but I usually go see them for Christmas every year. I have three sisters too. It can get pretty loud at family get-togethers."

"That seems nice. I always wanted siblings, but my mom died when I was a baby, and that was it for my dad. He never even looked at another woman the rest of his life. Can you imagine loving someone *that* much?" I regret it as soon as I ask. Not because I'm worried I'm making the mood too heavy, but it feels weird to talk about *love* and everything when things are so... well, whatever they are with Ten. Does he think I'm hinting at something?

I squirm and sneak a glance at him to find him watching me with a hint of curiosity in his eyes.

"As weird as this is going to sound, that seems...*nice*." He looks down and then back at me, a vulnerability in his eyes that makes my heart beat faster. "Not the dying part, obviously."

"Of course." I smile and try to sound as normal as I can, so he won't notice just how much the way he keeps looking at me affects me.

While we finish eating, he tells me more about his sisters and what it was like growing up with them. And when we're done, he makes a move to stand up to take his dishes to the kitchen, but I catch him wincing again. I scramble to my feet and snatch his plate and empty cup.

"Let me take these."

"You don't have to," he insists, but I ignore

him.

"Oh, hey, would a massage help?"

Ten's eyes lock on mine and heat passes between us. "A massage would be great."

CHAPTER 14

TEN

My heart rages as Bambi follows me into my bedroom. Fuck, which one of us is supposed to be the virgin here? I've had dozens of guys in my bedroom, actually, probably fewer than that because having strangers in my bed sounds gross, so we don't often make it farther than the couch. But the point stands. He's hardly the first man who has stood just inside the door to my bedroom, casually looking around at the clutter on various surfaces, my unmade bed, my pile of dirty clothes in the corner.

It *is* the first time I've wondered what the man is thinking. Does Bambi like my bedroom? Is he nervous? Does he want to give me a *just* massage, or was it a line like Lux suggested I use?

Bambi crosses my room and picks up a little surfboard-shaped keychain Trick gave me for my birthday last year and runs his thumb over the smooth surface before setting it down. He touches a few more random items, his exploration of my room feeling strangely intimate.

After a minute or so, he turns back toward me. "You have to take your shirt off."

His forwardness shocks the hell out of me until I remember that he's talking about giving me a massage. I step closer to him, dipping down to run my nose along his throat and against his jaw while reaching around him to grab a bottle of massage oil out of my dresser. Bambi's breath hitches and he sways into me, his reactions to every touch so genuine and fucking addictive.

My cock stiffens and aches as I imagine what it will be like to strip him naked for the first time and kiss every inch of his body until he's squirming and begging for more. I press a kiss to the sharp angle of his jaw and then force myself to pull back before I push him too far, too fast.

He looks dazed as I put the bottle of oil into his hand and then take another step back, yanking my shirt over my head and tossing it onto the floor. I shove my shorts down next, careful not to tweak my back too much as I kick them off, leaving me standing in nothing but my tight, white briefs.

"Maybe I should take my clothes off too," Bambi says, his eyes greedily devouring every inch of bare skin I've exposed. "You know, so they don't get all oily."

"Massage oil is very caustic for clothing," I

agree, barely managing to keep a straight face.

There's a noticeable tremble in his hands as he grabs the hem of his shirt and tugs it over his head, dropping it next to mine. The bulge in the front of his shorts mirrors mine, straining against the thin material.

But his very obvious and drool-worthy erection isn't the only thing keeping me staring. I've seen Bambi on the beach once or twice, wearing his swim trunks, but I never really stopped and *looked* before. He's small, petite even, but he's not all skin and bones. He's sturdy, all lithe muscles and extra padding in just the right places.

"Fuck, you're sexy," I murmur, reaching out to drag my fingers down the trail of dark-blond hair that extends from his belly button, disappearing under his shorts. He shivers, his cock jerking.

Mine throbs in return, desperate to be closer to him. Fuck, it's hard to take it slow when all I want to do is toss him down on the bed and debauch the hell out of him.

"If you keep looking at me like that, you won't get your massage," he warns, his voice shaky, his eyes fixed on mine.

"Okay," I agree, my voice coming out low and gravely. Except, shit, no, taking it slow. Unless...is that his way of hinting that he's ready for more than kissing? Should I just ask? That seems like the adult thing to do.

Bambi chuckles, putting a hand pressed to the middle of my chest and giving me a gentle push. "Lie down so I can massage you. You're going to hurt yourself if you keep thinking that hard."

"Hey." I protest his teasing but grin as I follow his instructions and climb onto the bed, lying down on my stomach, tucking my arms under my head.

The bed bounces as Bambi climbs on and then crawls up my body until he's straddling my ass. The weight of his body and the unmistakable press of his erection makes my hole ache and my cock throb, pinned against the bed.

Jesus, my body really is slutty as fuck. I need to find five-hundred percent more chill, or I'm going to end up embarrassing myself during this massage by coming in my underwear. The click of the massage oil cap doesn't help, sounding *way* too much like I'm about to get fingered and fucked. That's some Pavlovian shit right there.

It takes all of my willpower not to grind on the bed in search of relief for my cock, or to thrust my ass against Bambi until he's tempted to put us both out of our misery.

I draw in a sharp breath when a drizzle of cool oil touches my skin.

"Sorry," he says, his warm hands counteracting the chill of the oil as he uses both of them to spread it around.

"No worries. It's better than cold lube, at least."

Bambi laughs, working magic with his hands now as they glide over my back, zeroing in on all of the tense spots and knots. I relax into his touch, soft groans falling from my lips every so often when he hits a particularly tight spot.

Damn, he's good at this. My cock is still painfully hard, but the massage is so relaxing, I'm able to forget about sex for a while.

"So, do you get a lot of massages from guys?" he asks after working magic with my muscles for twenty minutes or so.

"Huh?" I murmur and then moan again when he uses his palm to work a particularly painful knot loose.

"You have oil on hand, so you must get a lot of massages." There's the slightest edge of jealousy in his voice that he's trying valiantly to restrain. It's way cuter than it should be.

"I spring for professional massages over at the resort sometimes. But no, none of the guys

I've hooked up with have given me a massage."

"They haven't? Why do you have a bottle of oil on hand then?"

"For jerking off," I answer simply. Bambi gasps, his hands slipping over my slick skin. His chest collides with my back before he catches himself, and as he wiggles around to re-seat himself, his erection finds its way between my ass cheeks, only a few thin layers of fabric between us. Even through them, I can feel the heat of his cock between my cheeks.

"For...?"

"Masturbation, Bambi. I assume you're familiar?" I tease, my mind going back to the morning when I spotted the dildo on his bed.

He laughs breathlessly. "Yes, I'm familiar with masturbation." He moves his hands slower over my back, a feeling of anticipation reverberating between us as I wait to see if he's going to say anything else about it. If the door is open or if I should steer the conversation back to something more innocuous.

"Can I tell you something?" he asks.

BAMBI

"Of course," Ten says, his voice relaxed and slightly muffled by his position.

I must be crazy to even consider this confession, but with him lying under me, relaxed from the massage, his skin slick and oiled, warm from my touch, I feel like I want to tell him something personal, something I wouldn't tell anyone else.

"A few weeks ago, I bought my first sex toy." I slide down so I'm straddling his thighs, and I focus my attention on his lower back more now.

"Oh yeah?" he asks and then groans as I dig my thumbs into his taut muscles. My cock jerks at the sound. Is that what he sounds like during sex? I really want to find out.

"But I haven't worked up the courage to use it properly," I admit.

"What do you mean? You've used it as a rolling pin instead of for getting off or something?" he jokes, and I snort a laugh.

"No, like, I haven't...put it inside myself." My cock tingles and aches. I can't believe I'm having such an open conversation about masturbation with *Ten*. More than that, I have my hands all over him, and the way he was looking at me before I started the massage...it's like he wants me, *really* wants me.

"What do you do with it instead?" he asks, his voice husky. He lifts his hips slightly, and I wonder if he's as hard as I am and what it would feel like to reach under him with my oil-slick fingers to feel the heat and weight of his erection in my hand.

My heart beats faster, heat pooling in the pit of my stomach and precum leaking from my cock to make my shorts damp and sticky. I don't want to chicken out. I don't want to.

Do it. Be brave.

My pulse thunders so loudly in my ears I can hardly hear myself think as I bravely slip my trembling hand under Ten. The sound of him gasping breaks through the rush of my heart in my ears and makes my cock even harder.

He lifts his hips a little more, making it easier for me to slide my hand inside his briefs, my whole body shuddering at the first brush of my fingertips over his scorching hot, silky erection.

"I hold the toy against my cock and kind of...." I lick my lips, trying hard to catch my breath as I slowly explore the shape of his erection. It's true. It is pierced, and not just the kind that's through the head. I drag my fingers along his shaft, counting the barbells through the underside. "Hump it," I finish, and Ten makes a throaty sound.

"Fuck, Bambi, you're killing me."

My fingers reach the head of his cock, which is dripping with precum. "Do you want me to stop?" I ask, too turned on to even be embarrassed by the tremble in my voice.

"Don't you dare." He moans as I finally wrap my hand fully around his cock, scooting forward again until my erection presses against the curve of his ass.

I absently reach for the waistband of his briefs with my free hand, and he lifts his hips again as if inviting me to take them off. Fuck, am I really doing this? What even is *this*?

Does he want me to fuck him? The pit of my stomach quivers with desire and anxiety in equal measure. Ten must sense it because, in a heartbeat, he's rolling to his back, a relaxed, slack expression on his face, even with his eyes full of fire and lust.

Now I'm on top of him, face to face, his underwear half pulled down in the front, the head of his cock peeking out, dark with arousal and glistening with a mix of his precum and the massage oil I just rubbed all over it.

He hooks his fingers in the waistband of my shorts and slips them down my hips, taking my nervous inhibitions with them as my erection bobs free. I tug his underwear farther down as well. Ten grabs the bottle of oil, pours some more into his hand, and then tosses it aside and grabs my hip with his free hand to coax me closer.

I can't stop staring at our cocks, nearly touching, both so hard we're visibly throbbing. I've never been this turned on in my life, a shiver wracking my body as he reaches for our erections and takes them both in his oiled grasp.

"Oh my god," I pant.

"Is this okay?" he asks as I fall forward, bracing my hands on the bed on either side of his head.

"Yes," I gasp, thrusting into the tight tunnel of his hand, the feeling of his cock trapped against mine a million times better than the dildo because I can feel the heat coming off him. I can feel his pulse in all of his bulging veins, the skin-warmed metal of his barbells adding an extra texture that has my toes curling and my eyes rolling back. "Ten, I can't...oh my *god*," I groan again, dropping my forehead to his.

"I've got you, Bambi." His voice sounds just as wrecked as mine, his hand moving over our dicks faster and faster.

I can't help myself from thrusting against him, even though I keep throwing off his rhythm. He doesn't seem to mind though. Our mouths bump each other, too messy and imperfect to be considered kissing, but somehow even better that way.

Ten's tongue flicks over my bottom lip, the coarse hair of his legs dragging against mine, my fingers twisting the bed sheets as his free hand hooks around my neck.

"Ten," I moan and pant. "Ten, *Ten*."

"Fuck, Bambi. Give it to me, baby. I want to feel you come against my cock. I want to see you fall apart for me." I'm not sure if it's the desperate, strained quality of his voice or the way he drags his thumb over the head of my cock just right on the next stroke, but I don't have any choice but to give him exactly what he wants.

I let out a strangled cry and hump more wildly into his grasp, spilling my release all over his cock. He moans too, the sound muffled as I slam my mouth to his, unable to catch my breath as my orgasm racks me. I'm not sure if an orgasm can be so good you die from it, but what a way to go.

Even once I'm oversensitive, my balls empty and sore from coming so hard, I can't stop moving against him, desperate to memorize the feeling of his cock pulsing out his orgasm, the filthy, wet, sticky feeling of being covered in our releases.

Eventually, I collapse on top of him, both

of us dragging in ragged breaths.

"Holy hell, Bambi. That was the best sex of my life," he pants, wrapping his arms around me, smearing more of the oil and cum over my back, but I'm too exhausted to care.

My stomach squirms again, less pleasantly this time than it did earlier. "You don't have to say that. I know that wasn't *real* sex, and I know this probably doesn't mean anything. It's okay, I promise."

That was by far the best experience of my life. The last thing I want to do is get greedy by thinking it means more than it does.

"Hey," Ten says with a stern edge to his voice. I tilt my head so I can look at him. "First of all, what is *real* sex? That felt pretty damn real to me, and anal isn't the end-all. Got it?" I nod, stunned to hear him say that. A warm feeling spreads through my chest as he holds my gaze. "And second, I don't know what *this* is. I know it's complicated because you aren't sure if you're staying, and I don't have the first damn clue what I'm doing."

I nod again, my heart sinking this time. "I know. It's okay, I—"

He cuts me off with a hard kiss. "I don't know what this is," he says again. "But it's *not* nothing."

Maybe you can't die from a too-good orgasm, but can you die from a man like Ten saying something that perfect? It feels like you could die from it, and it's officially the way I want to go.

CHAPTER 15

TEN

"That shirt looks great," I say, but the words are barely out of my mouth before he's pulling it over his head and tossing it onto the pile with three others. "You realize you're running out of options, right?" I grin as he grabs the second to last T-shirt out of his dresser. "It's just a beach party. No one cares what you're wearing."

He shoots me a disgruntled look that I have to bite the inside of my cheek to keep from laughing at.

"It was bad enough going to these things before, but now everyone's going to be looking at me as your boyfriend, or whatever." He gives me another nervous look out of the corner of his eye as if he's waiting for me to correct his use of the word *boyfriend*. I'm not sure if that's what we are, but it's damn nice to hear it on his lips, so I'm not about to worry over semantics.

"They're likely to be too drunk to look at you any kind of way," I tell him with amusement as he tugs off that shirt and settles on the final option in the drawer.

"I know. I just don't want to look ridiculous. I want to look at least a *little* bit like the kind of guy who should be with you." He glances down at himself and frowns, but considering he's out of options, he doesn't remove this one.

I step into his bedroom and stride over to him, wrapping my arms around him from behind and tucking my face into the crook of his neck. "That's ridiculous. Have you *seen* you?"

He makes a *tsk* sound between his teeth and then gasps when I nip at the side of his neck. Bambi tilts his head, giving me more access to his throat, and I smile against his skin.

"It's going to be fun. The guys will probably be nosy as fuck and obnoxious about the fact that we're...whatever we are. But then they'll get it out of their system, and we'll all have a good time. If all goes *really* well, you'll get so stoned you try to drown yourself."

He huffs out a laugh. "You're never going to let me live that down, are you?"

"Never," I tease, pressing one more kiss to his neck and then slipping my fingers through the belt loop on the back of his jeans to drag him away from his dresser before he pries open a hidden compartment full of even more shirts.

"Okay, okay, I'm ready. Let's do this," he

says.

I drag him all the way through the house by his jeans, both of us laughing by the time we reach the front door when I finally let him go to grab the keys for my golf cart.

"I just put some new string lights on this baby. I want to show her off," I explain with a grin, and Bambi laughs again.

"You guys are absurd with your carts. Did you see all the new flamingos Boston put on his? It's out of hand."

"It's fun." I shrug, letting the front door bang closed behind us as we head out and hop onto my newly decorated cart. I decided on a whole new theme, actually, not just the lights. *Peacocks*. It's perfect, and I really think I nailed the tail feathers. The teal-and-blue lights are the ideal accent to the whole aesthetic.

The evening air is still warm, but it carries on it the slightest tease of cooler nights ahead. As I pull the cart out onto the street, Bambi's hand falls on my thigh, and I smile again, a warm feeling rushing through my chest.

It's been three days since the massage and all the delicious, filthy things that happened after, and I have no doubt my friends are going to harass us about it tonight. I haven't told them any specifics. I'm not really sure what the protocol is on hooking up with someone you actually *like*. I've never thought twice about giving them all the juicy details on hookups with tourists. I'm usually a little stingier with info when I've fooled around with another local, but I'm still not too shy about spilling it. But with Bambi...

I glance over at him as I drive down the quiet street, passing a few other people heading to the beach on foot.

The idea of gossiping with the guys about the way his hands felt on my body, the size of his cock, the taste of his lips, it feels wrong. For the first time, I want to keep that moment to myself, share it only with Bambi and know it's just for us.

We picked a more accessible beach tonight, one that doesn't require us to cut behind any houses to get to. When the raging fire and small crowd of locals come into view, I pull my cart up along the side of the road and turn it off.

"Come on, Bambi. Let's go play." I hop off and then stop to wait for him to do the same, holding my hand out to him without giving it a second thought.

He hesitates for a second, looking at my hand and then at everyone congregating a few yards away around the fire. My heart sinks. I might not give a shit about the ribbing we're no doubt about to get, but maybe he'd rather keep things more under wraps to avoid all of the teasing and prying.

I start to drop my hand, but Bambi finally catches it.

"Let's go get a drink," he suggests, giving my hand a squeeze. I grip him back and nod.

When we arrive at the party, it's obvious we're a little late. Easy and Trick greet us with a drunken shout of welcome, Lux reaching into the nearest cooler to pull out a pair of beers for us.

"Thanks, man." I take them both and hand one to Bambi.

"Could the two of you be any fucking cuter holding hands and shit?" Easy teases, smirking at our joined hands while I expertly use my belt buckle to get the top off my bottle.

"Jealous?" I taunt, taking a swig.

Bambi drops my hand so he can open his own.

"No, but dying to hear all the juicy details. Tell me, Bambi, has Ten's kissing technique improved, or is he as sloppy as ever?"

Trick chuckles, and Bambi blushes before a wicked smirk spreads over his face.

"He's better than your dad," he ribs to a round of *oohs* and *damns* from not only Trick and Lux but Boston, Devil, and Angel, who are nearby as well.

"Did you just hit me with an *I fucked your dad* joke?" Easy looks shocked.

"Simple, yet elegant. I like it." I swoop in and kiss Bambi's cheek, feeling it warm under my lips as he blushes again, this time without a hint of shyness in the cocky smile he keeps on his face. I like this confident, snarky version of him. Who knew all it would take was some oiled-up frotting?

"The point goes to Bambi this round," Trick declares. "Now, the question is, how many drinks will it take to *finally* get Bambi to tell us the answer to the question we're all wondering."

"What question is that?" I ask, arching an eyebrow at him.

Trick smirks back. "How many donuts?"

They cackle, and I start considering other options for best friends.

The fire crackles merrily and the noise from the party finds a way to harmonize with the sound of the waves a dozen or so yards away, creating a mesmerizing sort of cacophony all around us.

I sip my beer, but Bambi seems to be on a different plan, downing one and then reaching for another. I'll keep an eye on him tonight so he can let loose and have fun. I don't mind tucking a drunk little deer into bed later. I just don't want to pull him out of the ocean again.

Goose slips over to join our group, falling into a literal dick-measuring competition with Easy as they talk about a few of their noteworthy hookups from the tourist season while Bambi finishes off another drink and grabs a third.

"Can I ask you a question?" Bambi turns his big eyes in my direction a little while later, a hint of haziness in them, reflected in the firelight as he sways a little on his feet thanks to the alcohol he's been downing.

"Shoot." I slip the half-empty bottle out of his hand and finish it so he doesn't get the chance to.

"What's with the duck donut...?" He scrunches up his forehead in confusion. "Donut dunk," he tries again, and I chuckle.

"Dick measurement by way of donut?" I guess, and he nods. I grin, feeling a little silly explaining it, but he seems to be drunk enough that he may not remember it later anyway. "There was this one night approximately a million years ago when we stopped by the donut shop while Easy was closing up, and there were all these leftover donuts that needed to be thrown out and, well...one thing kind of led to another."

Bambi's mouth forms into an adorably

shocked little O, his eyes going wide. "You put the donuts on your dicks?"

"We did. And let me tell you, it is *not* easy to keep an erection while your friends are laughing and chucking donut chunks at you in the process."

He laughs, and I join him, considering how ridiculous it sounds when I actually explain it.

"I'll tell them you have a five-donut dick if you want me to," he leans in and whispers near my ear.

I chuckle and loop an arm around his middle, then turn my head to steal a kiss because I simply can't help myself.

BAMBI

As soon as Ten's mouth touches mine, the drunk haze fades a bit and my whole body heats up. I wrap my arms around his neck and pull him deeper into a kiss, slipping my tongue between his lips and pressing myself against him.

I'm so absorbed in the kiss I only barely hear Goose sigh from beside us. "I need to find someone to make out with."

When I finally break the kiss, I'm surprised to find that Boston has joined the circle, his arm around Goose, a suggestive smile on his lips.

"You rang?" he asks, waggling his eyebrows suggestively.

"Have fun with him. I know I did," Trick taunts, causing Boston to drop his flirtatious expression in favor of a frown before slinking away, muttering something about sloppy seconds and the island being too small.

"Liar," Goose says, shaking his head at Trick.

"Shh." He grins and puts a finger to his lips.

"Oh, I have an idea," Hen stumbles over, clearly as drunk as I am. "Let's play Spin the Bottle." He gulps down the remainder of his beer and then holds the empty bottle up.

I giggle and hiccup, and Hen gives me a playful look. "Come on, Bambi. Let us all get a shot at those pretty lips of yours."

Ten makes a rumbly sound beside me that almost sounds like a growl. My cock tingles and I lean into him, the sturdiness of his body making the world feel a little less unsteady around me.

"Sure, why not," I agree.

There are some giddy *whoops,* and everyone grabs more drinks before Hennessey leads the way over to the nearby boardwalk so we'll have a surface to spin the bottle on. I take a seat on the steps while everyone else finds their spot, gathering around in a small circle like a bunch of teenagers to see who will be kissing who tonight.

It feels juvenile and ridiculous and all kinds of fun. I don't know if it's the fire heating up the beach, the excessive amounts of alcohol I've guzzled way too quickly, or the fact that, for the first time in my life, I'm part of the easy banter and camaraderie of the group that has me feeling fuzzy and warm all over. Whatever it is, I like it.

"Me first," Easy declares, grabbing the bottle and setting it whirling with a flick of his wrist.

Even while it's spinning, a few more guys clamber up the stairs to join the group. Angel and Devil are drunk and laughing as they stumble up and squeeze into the circle, followed by Lyric—surrounded by a cloud of pot smoke—and finally Boston.

The bottle stops spinning on Hen, who scowls at Easy.

"Hell no, spin again," Hen says.

"Hey, that's not part of the rules. Play fair," Angel insists.

"Uh, yeah, I'm not about to get my tongue bitten off," Easy says, rubbing the back of his head and then reaching to spin the bottle a second time. This time it lands on Devil, who gives a deep chuckle before leaning across the circle to share a brief yet steamy kiss with Easy. Angel fans himself and then kisses his husband as soon as he sits back.

Devil takes his turn, and everyone cheers and laughs when the bottle lands on his husband. The two of them share a second heated kiss, full of tongue and groping. It goes around the circle like that for a while, kisses and the joint Lyric brought being swapped. I pass on the weed this time and join the rest of the group in gasping dramatically when Trick's spin lands on Boston.

"Finally, straight to the source, no more sloppy seconds," Trick taunts, puckering his lips at Boston, who scowls so deeply it's actually a little unsettling.

Surprisingly, he *does* lean across the circle, catching Trick by the front of the shirt. With Trick sitting right next to me, I hear his breath catching, whether it's because he's shocked that Boston is actually going to kiss him or he's truly afraid of the stormy look in the man's eyes, I'm not sure. Their mouths collide, but it's more of a rough bite than a kiss.

Boston sits back, still looking all ragey and annoyed, Trick seemingly out of taunts for the first time since I've known him. The bottle spins again, and this time it lands on me. I let out a startled laugh and look across at Boston, my boss. This is weird, right? But I can't *not* kiss him.

That's the rule of the game.

He snorts, his lips quirking in a half-smile as he leans in toward me. I close my eyes and pucker my lips, feeling awkward but amused by the game all the same. I just hope he doesn't bite me like he did Trick. That looked a little painful.

Before his mouth can meet mine, a pair of strong arms wrap around me from behind and I gasp as I'm hoisted into the air.

"Nope," Ten says, his voice sounding deep and rough. "Nope, nope, nope."

"What—" I try to get my bearings, the world spinning around me as he maneuvers me over his shoulder.

"Sorry, but Bambi's lips are mine until further notice, and I'm not really in a sharing mood."

Ten's words send a spike of heat through me. He doesn't want to share me? Not even for a childish kissing game? I ball the back of his shirt in my fists and laugh as he tromps down the boardwalk steps and carries me away, the rest of the group jeering and calling after us.

"Is this you carrying me off the beach thing going to become a tradition?" I ask.

Ten's laughter vibrates through me. "Possibly."

"Okay, cool. I don't mind. I just like to know what to expect."

When we reach the golf cart, Ten lowers me to my feet, my body sliding against his until I touch the ground. I don't step back, though, staying plastered to him as I look up into his eyes in the dim light.

"I feel cheated. I was supposed to get a kiss," I joke, and Ten takes the bait, putting his hands behind my head and pulling me in to claim my lips.

Best beach party ever.

CHAPTER 16

TEN

I'm up just after the sun for a change, barely able to contain myself as I slip quietly back into the house. I vaguely register that I'm tracking sand through the house, hurrying down the hallway to Bambi's bedroom, practically vibrating with excitement. The waves are *perfect* this morning, gentle but still present. The ideal conditions for a first-timer to climb on a board.

The thought of sharing Bambi's first waves with him has me so fucking giddy I can't stand it. I pause outside his bedroom, raising my hand to knock before deciding on a much more fun plan.

I quietly twist the knob and ease the door open, peeking my head inside. The morning sun is streaming through the window and bathing him in a golden light, his blond hair all trussed up. He has one pillow under his head, the other wrapped up in his arms, full cuddle mode engaged. My heart beats out an uneven rhythm, and for a few seconds, all I can do is stare at him.

When I finally shake myself out of it, a

wicked grin spreads over my face, and I take a running leap onto his bed. The wooden frame groans and the mattress springs creak, the whole thing bouncing under my weight. Bambi grunts, clutching his pillow tighter and then whipping his head around to figure out what's happening. His sleepy, confused expression might be the cutest fucking thing I've seen in my life as I crawl on top of him, pinning him to the bed.

"Morning, Bambi," I murmur with a grin, leaning in to nip at his earlobe.

"What time is it?" he asks, yawning and then squinting at the window like he's going to figure out the time from the angle of the sun.

"It's time to wake up," I answer vaguely, sure I won't get him out of bed if I reveal the actual hour. As an added incentive, I continue to kiss along the side of his neck.

He moans and pushes his ass back against me, coaxing my cock to swell. Damn, this is going in the wrong direction. Not that I don't love the idea of staying in bed and getting naked with Bambi, but the ocean is calling this morning.

He wiggles under me, getting his covers off and rolling over to face me. He frowns when his toes brush against my flip-flops.

"Why are you getting sand in my bed?"

"That's beach life, baby."

"I feel like I'm going to need a *lot* of coffee for whatever you have planned this morning."

I distract him from his grumbling with another kiss, this time fully claiming his mouth with mine. Bambi sighs into my lips, and I get that fluttery, heart-too-big feeling again.

Eventually, I manage to stop kissing him, and I jump out of his bed, dragging him up with me.

"Come on, I have presents for you," I tell him.

"Hold on, let me put some clothes on." He tries to go to his dresser, but I stop him, impatiently tugging him toward the door.

"You don't need clothes."

"I'm not doing naked beach yoga," Bambi says flatly, and I bark out a laugh. Yeah, I finally let him in on that favorite activity of mine.

"No public nudity, got it." I manage to coax him out of his bedroom, wearing only the incredibly distracting boxer briefs he slept in.

When we reach the kitchen, I pull out one of the chairs and motion for him to sit. I grab the iced coffee I made earlier out of the refrigerator and hand it to him, and then I go back outside to get the presents I picked up for him a few days ago.

With a wetsuit draped over my shoulder, I lean his brand-new surfboard against my golf cart and then jog back up the steps into the house.

"You got me a wetsuit?" he asks, taking it when I hold it out to him. "Oh, are we going surfing?"

"We're going surfing," I confirm. "The waves are perfect this morning."

A range of emotions flickers over his face, from excitement to nervousness. "Are you going to laugh at me if I suck at it?"

"If you knew how many times I slipped, hit my face on the board, and gave myself a black eye, you would be the one laughing," I confess. "It's your first time. It's okay if it takes you a while to get the hang of it. I just want to share my favorite thing with you."

A slow smile spreads over Bambi's face. He tugs his bottom lip between his teeth and nods quickly. "Okay." He gulps down some of his coffee and then sets the glass down on the table before standing up. "So do I just put this thing on over my underwear or what?"

BAMBI

There's a chill in the air this morning, reminding me that October is only a couple of days away. I'm surprised by how warm the wetsuit keeps me as I fall into the water for the dozenth time as I try and fail yet again to make it to a standing position.

"That was closer," Ten says encouragingly, paddling over to me and steadying my board so I can climb back on, spitting saltwater out of my mouth.

It takes me an embarrassing number of tries to drag myself back onto my board, my muscles all starting to get rubbery with exhaustion after an hour of trying to stay on my damn board when I stand up.

"Can we just float for a few minutes?" I ask once I finally manage to get up, sitting with my legs hanging off either side into the cool ocean water.

"Of course," Ten agrees, that easy smile of his making me feel like less of an idiot for being so bad at this.

He drags in a deep breath, tilting his face up toward the sun with an absolutely breathtaking expression of happiness and peace. For just a second, the thought that I could ever leave this place is absolutely ludicrous. Where else in the world could joy as pure as this exist?

Ten opens his eyes again and looks over at

me, his expression never changing as we both rise and fall with the gentle waves, slowly pushing us closer to the shore before pulling us back out.

"Are you about ready to call it?" he asks.

I open my mouth to tell him hell yes, I've had enough punishment for one day. But I surprise myself. "Let me try just one more, then we can go."

"Let's do it," he agrees.

I lean forward, lying against the board like he showed me, and we both paddle toward the oncoming waves. All of Ten's instructions run through my mind one after another, crowding each other out as I try to remember exactly how he told me to do this. I take a quick glance over at him and see that same look of relaxed happiness, every motion he makes fluid and unconscious. He's not thinking about what he's going to do next. It's like he's one of the waves in the ocean, just doing what comes naturally.

I bring my attention back to my own body, my own board, and I push away all of the instructions cluttering my mind, focusing instead on the shape of the wave that's getting close, the way it rises out of the ocean to greet me.

I grip my board and pop up in one smooth movement, finding purchase with my feet this time. My whole body wants to tense as soon as the wave catches my board, but I force myself to stay loose, to move with the ocean instead of trying to fight it. And then it feels like I'm flying, riding the waves and becoming one with them. Holy shit, Ten was right. This is the most incredible feeling in the world.

I let out a whoop, and I hear an echoing one from Ten.

"I did it!" I shout, my legs trembling under me when I finally lower myself back down.

"You did." Ten sounds breathless as he paddles over to me. "You were amazing."

I expect him to stop a few feet short, but he keeps coming until he's close enough to reach over and drag me in for a kiss, nearly pulling me off my board in the process.

Just like always, his mouth tastes like salty ocean and sunshine. I can feel the shape of his smile against my lips, and I answer it with my own, my heart going wild from the adrenaline of what I just did and the addictive feeling of Ten's kiss. I've never felt so alive in my entire life. If I could, I would bottle this feeling and live off it until I die.

We finally break the kiss and make our way back to the beach, dragging our boards into the wet sand. I feel like a live wire, my body vibrating, laughter bursting from my lips.

"I can see why you like this. I feel so..." I don't even have words for it, so I let out a shout of joy.

Ten smiles at me, his eyes soft around the edges when they meet mine. After a second, he tears them away, glancing one way up the beach and then the other. From the look of things, we're the only ones on this stretch of beach this morning.

Just like he did in the house this morning, he snags my wrist and starts to drag me down the beach.

"You really like to manhandle me, don't you?" I tease, my heart tripping with excitement.

"Only because I can tell you like it," he says, looking back at me as he pulls me toward a row of outdoor shower stalls. My skin prickles and my cock makes an attempt to swell inside the too-tight material of my wetsuit. Ten's eyes darken as if he can see the arousal written all over my face. Maybe he can.

I quicken my pace, not pausing for a second as he pulls me into the farthest stall. There aren't any doors. The cement half-walls separating each shower are the only thing keeping us from being fully exposed to anyone who might wander down to this part of the beach.

I greedily launch myself at him, his arms catching me as our lips collide. I wrap my legs around his waist and Ten slams me against the back wall, the only full wall in the otherwise outdoor shower. The man is an expert multitasker, holding me up with one hand, his other finding the zipper on the back of my wetsuit, all while his tongue slides over mine, tangling and teasing.

Meanwhile, I can barely remember to breathe and kiss at the same time. I'm dizzy and beyond desperate. Frantic to taste more of him, to feel every inch of his body, to somehow be consumed by him.

All of the feelings well up inside me until I let out a muffled cry against his mouth. He pulls away from the wall enough to unzip me all the way, and then he sets me down. I reluctantly let my feet touch the cool, sandy cement.

The kiss breaks, and Ten is breathing as heavily as I am, his eyes wild and fiery, his chest heaving. A smile dances across his kiss-swollen lips. He puts his palm over the straining bulge in my wetsuit, my cock pushing painfully inside the sticky rubber.

"Fuck, I want to put my mouth on you, but I feel like I need to make it more special. Your first time getting a blowjob shouldn't be standing up in an outdoor shower, right?"

I'm only half-listening, all of my attention stuck on the phrase *put my mouth on you.*

"Oh my god. Please, please, please." I start to struggle out of the suit, Ten's hands joining mine only a few seconds later.

"I can take you home first," he offers, sounding a little helpless as he pushes the suit down around my waist as I start to wiggle out of it, his actions completely at odds with his weak protest.

"Here's good," I insist, moaning when my cock is freed, filling rapidly until it's standing straight up in front of me, hard and aching.

Ten moans, too, his eyes glued to my cock as if he's never seen it before. It's been a week since the first time, and I've been all over him every chance I've had, humping him constantly like I'm in heat.

The pit of my stomach tightens as he pushes me back against the wall, the showerhead right next to me. He drops to his knees in front of me, and my legs start to tremble. He wraps his hand around the base of my cock, and I clutch at the smooth wall.

Ten pumps my cock slowly, his fingers tightening a little on each upstroke and then loosening again, pulsing all around me maddeningly.

"Bambi," he murmurs, his eyes locked on mine as I struggle not to let them fall closed. I don't want to miss this.

"Ryan," I correct, and his smile changes, going from feral to...something else. My heart jolts and my body quakes. I reach out to brace myself on his shoulders, unable to stop myself from thrusting into his grasp.

"Ryan," he says, his voice as rough as gravel. He leans forward, his lips parting and then pressing the head of my cock with a gentle kiss.

My breath catches and my balls tighten, a bead of my precum clinging to his lips when he pulls back. My cock jerks hard, the heat in the pit of my stomach burning so hot I'm sure I'm about to lose it already. That would be just like me to ruin my first blowjob by coming all over his face before he even gets his mouth on me.

Fuck, that would still be hot.

I moan and thrust toward him, my cock brushing his lips again. He opens his mouth, the wet heat of it dragging against the length of my shaft. Electricity shoots up my spine, and I reach for his head, tangling my fingers in his short hair. I pull back and thrust toward his mouth again. This time he wraps his lips around me.

The warmth of his mouth sends another

wave of pleasure through me. I don't even know how it's possible that I haven't come yet, but every drag of his tongue along my shaft as he swallows me feels like an orgasm of its own.

I hit the fleshy back of his throat, and he tightens around me as he gags.

"Sorry," I mutter, jolting myself out of my lust haze and trying to pull out.

Ten grunts around me, grabbing my ass with both hands, forcing me to shove my cock into his throat again. This time he relaxes, swallowing and taking me even deeper. It's so hot, so fucking good.

I grip his hair harder, letting out a half-bitten-off cry as my cock pulses inside his throat. He moans, and the vibrations shoot through me, intensifying my orgasm tenfold. I pull my hips back and thrust deep again, lost to the sensation of spilling down his throat.

He kneads my ass cheeks and takes me over and over until I'm spent, barely able to hold myself up. I sag on the wall, and Ten gets to his feet, wrapping his arms around me to keep me standing.

He ducks his head to kiss me, gently this time. The bitter flavor of my cum on his lips sends a tremor through me.

When I manage to catch my breath and get

the feeling back in my legs, he reaches over to start the shower. I kick my wetsuit the rest of the way off and step under the lukewarm spray. Behind me, Ten strips out of his suit. I glance over my shoulder to admire the view of him naked from head to toe, his upper body covered with tattoos and muscles, his thighs thick from all of his favorite sports.

His cock is hanging hard between his legs, too heavy to stand up fully, so it swings with every movement he makes. Ten steps closer again, wrapping his arms around me, his body pressed to mine. The water on my skin wets him quickly. His cock is hard and throbbing against my ass cheek.

I gasp and thrust back into him, desperate to feel his cum coating my skin.

"Is it always like this?" I ask.

Ten drags his mouth along the crook of my neck while he grinds lazily against my ass like he's in no particular rush for this to end. He laughs and nips at my skin.

"This intense," I clarify.

"No. It's not always like this." His voice is raw and strained as he thrusts faster.

I turn my head a little more, and our mouths find each other. I brace my hands on the wall and imagine for a second that he's thrusting inside of me instead of just grinding on me. I moan into his lips, and he makes a similar, strangled sound.

His cum covers my skin in hot bursts, his thrusts stuttering and his lips stilling against mine.

The now-cold shower water washes it away too quickly, leaving the two of us panting and shivering until I finally get the wherewithal to reach over to shut it off.

"Oh shit, I just realized it probably hurt your back to lift me like that." It occurs to me that I've probably been letting him carry me around *way* too much, always hauling me away from the beach like some sort of sexy, possessive caveman.

He nuzzles my wet shoulder, nipping it gently. "Worth it. You can always give me another massage later if it seizes up."

"Deal," I laugh. "So, *that's* surfing?" I joke, and Ten lets out a breathless laugh.

"Pretty much."

"I want to surf every day," I say.

His eyes meet mine, something silent and heavy passing between us.

"Okay."

CHAPTER 17

TEN

Our wetsuits lay discarded on the sandy cement floor while the two of us finish rinsing the cum and saltwater off our bodies. When I reach around Bambi to shut off the water, he leans into my body. My heart jolts and I lean in to brush another kiss to his bare shoulder.

He bends down to pick up his wetsuit, holding it like he's going to put it back on.

"It'll be a pain in the ass. I'm riding back naked," I say, flinging mine over my shoulder, along with my soggy underwear.

Bambi raises both eyebrows, looking at me and then at the golf cart and back again before shaking his head and smiling. "You're corrupting me." He puts his suit over his shoulder too.

I chuckle, and we both grab our boards, heading back up the nearby boardwalk to where I parked the golf cart. I strap our boards to the roof, careful not to fuck up my peacock decorations.

When I slide bare-assed into the driver's seat, I take a second to just stare at how fucking incredible Bambi looks, water glistening on the miles of exposed skin he's rocking, the sun hitting him just right, like it did when he was asleep in bed this morning. How the hell have I never noticed how the sun hits a guy before? Has something changed with me, or is it just Bambi?

He glances over at me with a relaxed smile curving his lips, and my whole body warms. Maybe it *is* just Bambi.

"What now? Do you have cliff diving or something planned for us, or can I go home and take a nap after all that excitement?" he asks and then yawns.

"No cliff diving," I answer. "Shit, what day is it though?"

He frowns, dragging his fingers through his messy, wet hair. "Um, Thursday? I think?"

These are the real-life island problems no one ever warns you about. Time ceases to exist in all its forms, and it's even worse during the off-season.

As if to answer my question, my phone vibrates on the seat next to me. I pick it up to see a text in a brand-new group thread that includes Lux, Easy, Trick, Goose, and Hennessey.

HEN: We're still meeting at the carousel in an hour, right?

EASY: Yup.

HEN: Ugh, fuck off.

HEN: Sorry, reflex.

HEN: Someone better come help me with the paint because no fucking way am I carrying all these cans up the mountain alone.

GOOSE: I've got you. We have a lot, though, so we'll probably need everyone to grab a couple.

TRICK: I've been getting in some daily pushups. I'll take like six cans up the mountain. *flexes*

BOSTON: Careful, Trick might stick his dick in them.

TRICK: Fuck, I didn't even know you were in this text group.

BOSTON: I'm everywhere, motherfucker.

TRICK: *fatherfucker

LUX: Children, let's play nice. We can all come to your place, Hen, and load up our carts with paint.

STORM: Why was I added to this text?

HEN: Shit, sorry, Chef, I must've added you by accident.

GOOSE: I'm at Tea Bagged right now, and Raven says he's in.

TEN: Just took Bambi surfing. We've gotta run back to the house to get dressed, and then we'll meet you.

The next text that comes through is from Easy, a Star Wars meme about this whole operation being my idea. I chuckle and show Bambi.

"Paint for what?" he asks.

"You'll see." I grin at him while my phone vibrates with another text.

GOOSE: You're surfing naked these days? I need to spend more time at the beach.

HEN: Keep it in your pants, lol!

TRICK: Or don't;)

BOSTON: Uggggggh. Everyone keep it in their pants and, Ten, go put some damn pants on. I'm muting this thread. See you all at Hen's in a bit.

A string of 'goodbye' trickles in, and I mute the thread as well, finally starting the cart up and heading toward home.

BAMBI

When we get back to the house, we hang our wetsuits out to dry and get dressed. Ten plays coy, refusing to tell me what we're doing today, but since paint was mentioned, I put on my rattiest clothes. With this group, it could be anything from sprucing up some buildings in town to an all-out paint fight. Hen did say something about carrying paint up the mountain, but I really can't begin to guess.

On my way back through the kitchen, I stop at the refrigerator to grab a couple of water bottles for us, and I spot a pile of mail on the counter. I guess it came on the ferry yesterday. I'm not expecting anything other than junk mail, but I thumb through it quickly anyway just to check.

My heart sinks when I land on an envelope with the Columbia logo on it. A month ago, it felt inevitable that I would go back to finish med school, but now...

Ten walks into the kitchen fully dressed—what a shame—with a big grin on his face.

"Ready to hit it, Bambi?"

"Uh, yeah." I tuck the envelope back under the rest and put it out of my mind. I'll have to decide eventually, but today isn't the day. Today is whatever weird paint adventure Ten dreamed up for all of us. Today is about living in the moment...with my *friends*...with my boyfriend? Is that what Ten is? Is that what I want him to be?

"Everything okay?" he checks.

"Perfect." I force a smile even wider than his and hand him a water bottle. "Let's go before Boston kills Trick or Hen finally throttles Easy. Damn, there's a lot of drama around here, isn't there?"

Ten throws his head back and laughs. "So much fucking drama. But I love it."

"Me too," I admit.

We're the last ones to get to Hen's place, most of the paint already divvied up among each of the guy's golf carts.

Surprisingly, Storm is there, leaning against Boston's golf cart.

"Took you guys long enough," Hen teases, pushing a can of paint into my arms as soon as I'm close enough.

"We were, uh..." I glance at Ten, who's got that sexy, cocky smirk all over his face again.

"Surfing," he finishes for me, even though the look on his face makes it clear that isn't *all* we were doing.

Hen sighs. "It's been too damn long since I've *surfed*."

"Preach, brother," Goose agrees.

"Me three," Raven chimes in.

"There you go, Trick. Your next four-way is all sorted." Boston nods toward them.

"Perfect, easy pickins just the way I like." Everyone laughs at his retort, but as soon as the spotlight isn't on him anymore, I catch Trick's smile faltering quickly.

I wonder what the deal with that is. Clearly, I'm still *way* behind on island gossip.

We finish sorting out who's taking what. There are tons of paint supplies, so I'm guessing we're actually painting something and not just fucking around with it. Goose has a large toolbox on the seat of his golf cart, which makes me even more curious about what exactly the plan is for today. It's kind of fun not knowing, though, so I don't bother to ask.

A demanding meow breaks through the din of all of our conversations and laughter. We all quiet and turn to see Mr. Tubbs slinking out from around the side of Hen's house. He trots straight over to Storm and makes a little *mrrrow* sound, arching his head up for pets while rubbing himself on Storm's legs.

I've had very limited experience with the chef to this point, but he's never struck me as the friendliest man around. The few times I've been anywhere near the kitchen of his restaurant, I've heard him cursing loudly.

"Oh shit," Hen mutters as if he's expecting the man to punt the cat or something equally as dramatic. Instead, Storm stoops down to pet Mr. Tubbs, saying something to the feline that's too quiet for any of us to hear. The cat enjoys ear scritches for a few seconds before turning away, flicking his tail at all of us and trotting off again.

Storm straightens back up, his normal, tense expression back in place. "Are we doing this, or what?"

"Uh, yeah, I think we're all set," Hen says quickly, all of us awkwardly trying to pretend we didn't just see that sweet moment.

"Let's get at it," Ten says, clapping his hands together. Everyone divides up onto the available carts, Raven making space next to all of the paint on the back of Ten's, and we all take off through town toward the mountains.

If I thought our last hike was exhausting, I did not consider how much worse it would be while carrying cans of paint.

"Come on, Bambi, we're almost there," Ten encourages.

"Please kill me," I groan, which only receives a round of unsympathetic laughter from the rest of the group.

Ten slows his steps until he's right next to me and makes a grab for the two cans of paint I'm lugging.

"Give 'em," he says as I jerk them away.

"I'm just being dramatic. I can carry them."

He makes another grab for them, and I walk faster, laughing as I try to keep him from taking the paint from me, even though they really are heavy as fuck.

It's only a few more yards before we crash through the trees into the same clearing we found a few weeks ago, the carousel sitting in the sunshine, most of the flowers already wilted now, replaced by tall grasses.

"We're painting the carousel?" I ask, stopping in my tracks.

Ten shrugs. "I figured it could use a little TLC."

Goose heads straight for the control panel with his toolbox. "Let's see if I can get this baby working like new again."

He pops the panel open expertly like he's done it a million times. "He was an electrician before he moved here," Raven answers my unasked question.

"Seriously?" I squint at the free-spirited man with bright-blue hair today, the heavy scent of his soap surrounding him, no doubt from making a fresh batch this morning. "I cannot picture that."

Goose looks up and winks at me. "I'm an enigma."

"I'll say."

While he plays with the wiring, the rest of us start picking up paintbrushes and popping open paint cans. Shirts come off in a flurry like we're on a porn set instead of in a meadow.

Ten and I end up sharing a can of blue paint, working on a section together right near where we shared our first kiss. It's hard to believe that was less than a month ago. It's even harder to believe that Ten still seems to want me, seems to like me as much as I like him.

As if he can hear my thoughts, he stops painting and looks at me. Something heavy and tangible wordlessly passes between us for a few seconds.

"This is the damndest thing," Goose calls out, breaking my attention away from Ten. "This wiring is pristine. Someone must be out here doing maintenance on this without telling anyone. And it should be working fine, not all of this unreliable Start/Stop shit." He scratches his head.

"It's the ghooooooost," Easy jokes, waving his hands in a spooky manner while everyone laughs.

"Yup, good old Harold blessing soul mate unions or whatever," Boston agrees sarcastically.

"*None* of you guys believe?" Ten asks, disbelief dripping from his tone.

"I do," Raven says.

"None of the sane people here?" Ten reiterates, and Raven makes an indigent sound. Everyone exchanges looks, waiting to see if anyone will admit to believing in all of the ghostly, soul mate folklore of the island.

"What even is a soul mate?" Trick reasons with a shrug.

Ten scoffs. "When did all of you become so jaded and cynical? Sure, we're a bunch of sluts, but that doesn't mean we can't believe in love."

"Love and soul mates aren't the same thing," Easy says. "Soul mates are so..." He rubs the back of his neck, looking over at Lux as if he's hoping he'll help him out with what he's trying to say. "Woo-woo," he finally finishes.

Raven snorts. "Some things, some *people* have a destiny, even if you don't believe it."

"Oh yeah?" Hen challenges. "Was it destiny when I fell for Easy's bullshit and quit my job to stay here?"

"Yup," Raven answers easily. "You'll see eventually."

"Soul mates don't have to be romantic, do they?" Lux asks, and Easy looks at him again.

Raven gives him a mysterious smile but doesn't answer his question. I'm starting to think Hen is right, he likes having fun with his psychic schtick, but I'm not sure how real it is.

I glance over at Ten again. Then again, he *did* say that if I was open to new experiences, I'd find someone special. It doesn't get much more special than Ten.

The envelope waiting at home pops back into my mind. Maybe I should try asking Raven again what I'm supposed to do about it. There are two paths in front of me, and one of them was *so* clear before, and now I just don't know.

Ten pulls me out of my musings with a swipe of cold, wet paint against my cheek. I gasp, and he howls with laughter.

"Oh, you're going to get it." I dip my brush into the paint bucket and go after him.

Can I really leave all of this?

Can I really stay?

CHAPTER 18

TEN

"I need a shower. This paint is getting itchy," Bambi says with a laugh, picking at the drying blue paint on his skin as we step into the house.

I wrap my arms around him from behind and kiss his neck, loving the airy sound of his laughter. "Me too. We should really save some water by showering together."

Bambi chuckles again. "You are such a conservationist."

"I deserve a Nobel Prize," I agree solemnly.

He wiggles out of my grasp just long enough to turn around to face me. Our mouths crash together, the two of us stumbling down the hallway, laughing against each other's lips as we bang into the walls clumsily. Bambi teases his tongue against mine, the sweetness of his flavor coaxing my cock to harden.

Somehow, we manage to make it to Bambi's bathroom, breaking the kiss long enough for me to start the shower before falling back into it like our mouths are made of matching magnets. We work together to strip each other out of our paint-stained clothing.

"Do you think I could pull off a tattoo?" he asks, dragging his fingers along the rose on the lower part of my belly, tracing each petal delicately.

"You could pull off just about anything." I'm sure it sounds like a line, but I mean it. There's nothing that would make Bambi less addicting than he is. In addition to running a snorkel rental booth down by Turtle Fuck Cove, Trick is our local tattoo artist with a studio set up at his house for appointments. If Bambi wants to go, I'll be right there holding his hand.

"Maybe I'll put that on my island experiences list," he says lightly, but a shadow flickers over his expression.

I saw the envelope from the university when I brought the mail in, and I know he's seen it too, although I don't think he's opened it. Has he made a decision already? My heart beats heavily, my fingers tightening reflexively as if I can keep him right here with me if I just hang on hard enough.

His smile returns and he gives me a gentle shove in the direction of the shower. I pull back the curtain and step inside under the heated spray. Unlike the outdoor shower we shared this morning, the water is hot enough to steam up the air around us, Goose's soap providing some aromatherapy as it slowly melts, filling the air with the scent of lavender and sage. The man really is a wizard with soap.

Bambi joins me, crowding in under the stream of water, our bodies growing slick and slippery against each other. I reach for the bar of soap and lather it up between my hands, releasing even more of the soothing scent into the heavy air around us.

"I have another question," he says as I use my sudsy hands on his skin, gently scrubbing away at the streaks of paint on his arms and hands.

"Twenty-questions: The Shower Edition. I'm here for it."

He chuckles, the sound echoing off the walls. "It's dirty," he warns.

"In that case, you definitely have my attention."

Bambi turns around so I can get his back, and I take my time, working my thumbs into his neck and shoulder muscles until he moans and leans back into me.

"I've been wondering...but I wasn't sure when the right time to ask this particular question would be...I don't know if I'm just supposed to *know* somehow or how it usually works..."

"Bambi, just ask," I prompt.

"Do you top or bottom? Or, I mean, do you even like anal? I know not everyone does, so I probably shouldn't assume..."

"I like anal," I answer. "And I'm good with either." I let the water rinse the rich suds off his skin, and then I wrap my arms around him, plastering my front to his back, my hard cock pressing against the small of his back. I reach around to tease his hot, swollen shaft with my wet fingers, dragging them up and down his length slowly. "I love sinking inside a nice, *tight* hole." I thrust against him so he can feel how turned on I am. His breath hitches. "But I also love the breath-stealing, full feeling of being fucked, having my prostate pounded until I can't hold back from coming."

A whine slips from his throat. "Can I...?"

I make a low, rumbling sound in my throat. "You want to fuck me?"

He nods rapidly. "Please?"

"Since you asked so politely," I tease, releasing my hold on him so I can quickly wash myself off too. I don't linger on all of the spots of paint that are dried and tugging on my body hair. I'll worry about it later. Right now, I'm a lot more interested in what Bambi is offering.

I shut off the water and push the curtain back. I grab his towel off the hanging rack and do a cursory pat-down of my body, handing it to him to do the same. When he's done, he drops it on the floor in a heap, a wicked grin flashing over his face before he turns and sprints into his bedroom.

I'm right behind him, the two of us diving onto the bed. It creaks and groans, and I can still feel the grains of sand in the sheets from this morning. I make a mental note to give him fresh sheets when we're done so he doesn't have to sleep in a beachy mess.

We fall into another kiss, tussling and laughing into each other's mouths, our bodies hot and still slippery from the shower, our cocks hard between us.

"I can't believe you're going to let me fuck you," he murmurs breathlessly, greedily dragging his hands all over my body.

"Let you?" I scoff. "I'm prepared to beg if necessary."

He makes another breathless sound that strokes me deep inside and makes my cock ache. "I got lube and stuff the other day. Hold on."

Bambi rolls over and pulls open the drawer of his nightstand. I catch sight of the dildo tucked away in there, right next to his condoms and lube. He must spot it, too, because he pauses for a few seconds, his breathing speeding up.

"Grab it," I say gruffly.

BAMBI

I tear my eyes off my still unused dildo, shaking off the fantasy that started forming of watching it disappear inside of Ten until he's moaning and begging me to fuck him harder. I glance over my shoulder at him, sure I misheard what he meant. He was probably referring to the condoms and lube, right?

"It's a little bit smaller than your dick. It'll be a fun way to prep me," he says with a smirk, reaching past me to grab the dildo himself and dropping it on the bed between us.

"Fuck, that's hot." I snatch the lube and a condom out of the drawer as well and then slide it closed, shuffling back across the bed toward him.

My heart flutters and my skin heats and prickles with nerves, but Ten just lies there, one arm tucked casually under his head, his legs spread, his cock hard against his belly, looking relaxed and sexy as hell.

This has to be a dream, right? It's incomprehensible that the most gorgeous, perfect man

I've ever set eyes on in my life just asked me to prep him with my dildo and then fuck him. I reach down with my free hand and pinch my thigh just to check. I wince at the sharp sting of pain. Okay, not a dream.

I lick my lips and rake my eyes over the man in my bed. "Roll over," I say with an air of confidence that I am absolutely not feeling.

Ten raises his eyebrows at me, probably as surprised by the show of confidence as I am, and then rolls to his stomach, folding his arms under his head comfortably. His ass is an absolute work of art, round and taut, unmarred by the ink that covers most of his upper body. I settle between his spread thighs and grab his ass cheeks in both hands.

He lets out a low sound as I massage his cheeks and carefully part them to see the pucker of his hole. My cock jerks hard, a spike of heat going through me at the sight. His balls are big and full, pressed to the sheets, his hole tightening and relaxing under my gaze.

"Can I lick you?" I ask through a hoarse voice.

"Fuck," he groans, flexing his hips, humping the bed. "Please." His voice is raspy and desperate, sending a hot tremor through me.

With my fingers digging into his thick ass

cheeks, I lean in and drag the flat of my tongue from his balls up to his hole. We both moan. He tastes like lavender soap and clean skin, the slightest hint of musk underneath the stronger flavors.

My mouth waters and I lick him again, deeper this time, hungrier. His hole softens under my tongue, relaxing enough for me to shove it inside. Ten gasps and writhes, pushing his hips toward me in a silent plea for more.

I dig my fingers into his cheeks harder and nip at the rim of his hole, losing myself in the headiness of drawing desperate sounds from him and the feel of his pucker under my tongue. I'm vaguely aware of my cock throbbing and ignored between my thighs, my balls heavy and tight.

I sit back and wipe the back of my hand over my mouth, reaching for the dildo and lube. I squeeze the lube onto my fingers before smearing most of it on the head and shaft of the toy.

"Do you have a dildo that you use on yourself?" I ask, using my slicked fingers the same way I've just used my tongue, teasing them around his rim and then gently slipping one inside.

Ten pants, his inner muscles twitching around my finger, squeezing so tightly that my cock pulses jealously, desperate to sink inside and feel the same vice grip.

"Yeah. Sometimes I stick it to the shower wall and fuck myself until I come hands-free."

My brain nearly short circuits at that visual, a thick droplet of precum dripping from my cock onto the back of his thigh. I sink my finger a little deeper, spreading the lube around inside of him and moving it in and out a few times, mesmerized by the sight of it disappearing inside of him.

I'm suddenly extremely glad that he suggested the dildo to warm him up because there's a strong chance I'm going to come the second I get inside him. I ease my finger out and add a second. Ten spreads his legs even wider, bringing his knees under himself and raising his ass in a wordless plea to be fucked and filled.

I push my fingers deeper, finding a soft, fleshy spot that makes Ten grunt and gasp. How is it possible that of all the fantasies I've indulged in over the years involving Ten, I never once imagined how hot it would be to sink my fingers into him over and over, playing with his prostate and stretching his hole until it's relaxed and ready for more?

My lungs burn with my rapid breaths, my body trembling with all of the heat rushing through me. I ease my fingers out, and he sighs, the sound full of impatience. Picking the dildo back up, I use one hand to spread his ass cheeks again and notch the head of it against his glistening, relaxed hole.

He moans eagerly, the sound breaking off in a deep, guttural pitch as I ease the toy inside, my eyes fixed on the way his hole gives way to it. I push it in slowly until the balls press to his, his entrance stretched around it, his thighs quaking, and the muscles in his back twitching as he struggles to keep his hips still.

I run a hand along his back, pressing my throbbing erection against the curve of his ass cheek as I ease the dildo back out and then thrust it in faster this time.

"Yeah," he says breathlessly. "Give it to me."

My hand is trembling as I start to fuck him with it, trying to find the rhythm and angle that'll draw the best sounds from him, make his body flush and shiver. My precum drips over his skin, his moans getting louder and more desperate with every thrust.

"Fuck, Bambi, I'm so close," he pants. "Give me your cock. I want to finish with you inside me."

I groan and nearly come right on the spot, that hot feeling clenching around the pit of my stomach and drawing my balls up. I tug the dildo out of his ass, leaving his hole wet and gaping. My hands are so slick from the lube and trembling so badly that it takes me several tries to get the condom open, and I finally have to use my teeth to get the job done.

But if I thought getting it open would be the most difficult part, I was mistaken. I fumble in an attempt to get it on. I should have practiced on a banana or something first. Ten rolls to his back and smirks at me, snatching the condom from between my fingers, wrapping his free hand around the base of my cock, and rolling it on expertly.

"Come on, I want to see your face the first time you feel a tight ass squeezing your cock." He crooks a finger to beckon me closer.

I nod mutely and find my place between his legs. His thick thighs wrap around me as I blindly find his hole and push inside the same way I did with the dildo, bottoming out in one slow stroke.

Ten's eyelids flutter, his lips parting as an expression of utter bliss washes over his face. Even through the condom, I can feel the heat of his body, his inner muscles squeezing tightly around me.

I brace my hands on either side of his head, and we fall into a sloppy kiss. My movements as I fill Ten over and over are erratic and out of rhythm, but he doesn't seem to have any complaints about it. He rolls his hips to meet each thrust until I find a better rhythm. We pant and gasp into each other's mouths, Ten's hands stroking my back and grabbing my ass, his thighs flexing around me every time we rut together.

Sweat forms on our skin, adding to the dampness from the shower. Our tongues tangle and the bed creaks as I fill him over and over, his channel gripping my cock. My toes curl and the flicker of heat that started in my stomach earlier rages to a full inferno now.

"Right there," Ten groans against my mouth. "Harder."

I pull out and slam back into him harder, my vision whiting out at the rush of pleasure that rolls over me. He sucks and bites my lips, begging me to give it to him again, to fuck him harder until he lets out a strangled cry, his channel clamping down so tightly around me all of the air punches out of my lungs and my orgasm rushes through me without any chance of holding it back.

He wraps his arms around me, and I lose my rhythm again, thrusting haphazardly as his cum coats us both, the pulse of his muscles around my cock milking me until my balls are so empty they're sore and my entire body is buzzing and boneless.

I collapse on top of him, letting my spent cock slip from the vice grip of his ass as I nuzzle my face into the crook of his neck.

"Sorry I came so fast," I murmur, and he chuckles.

"I finished before you did."

"Oh yeah," I mumble stupidly.

We lie cuddled like that for a while, the rise and fall of his chest lulling me into a nearly unconscious state. Or maybe it's the fact that I just came harder than I ever have in my life. Eventually, I roll off him and dispose of the condom.

"I need to get you fresh sheets. These are all sandy," Ten says sleepily. "Unless..." He clears his throat. "Unless you want to sleep in my bed tonight."

My heart trips over itself, my stomach twisting in knots. Sleep in Ten's bed? Like, wrapped up in each other all night long like a real couple? He wants me to listen to his slow breathing as he falls asleep and then wake up the same way? Something tells me he's the kind of man who might reach for me in his sleep, as if he needs to reassure himself that I'm right there, still next to him, even when he's unconscious.

I swallow hard, my body full of terror and longing all mixed together and confusing as hell.

"The sheets would be good," I answer weakly. "I'm…um, I'm a light sleeper."

He cracks one eye open, studying me for a few silent seconds before nodding. "Fresh sheets it is."

Ten heaves himself out of bed. As he strides naked across the bedroom toward the door, my heart urges me to change my mind, to go crawl into his bed and let myself sink a little deeper into whatever this is. But my throat tightens, refusing to allow the words out.

If I fall into his bed now, I might never get back out.

What if it's already too late?

CHAPTER 19

BAMBI

"Help." I slam the still unopened envelope down on the counter at Tea Bagged.

I don't have to open it to know what's inside, another reminder that if I don't re-enroll, I'm going to lose my spot in the program, I'll have to reapply, I'll lose my scholarships. Basically, I'll be setting myself way, *way* back, possibly giving up everything I've dreamed of since I was a kid.

But some of my dreams are changing, and I can't figure out how to reconcile them all. Last night with Ten was...*everything*. But is it smart to give up the chance to be a doctor just because I'm falling for some gorgeous, incredible, perfect man?

"What's up, boo?" Raven asks, looking at the envelope and then back at me. "Am I supposed to put this to my forehead and guess what's inside?"

I huff. "Let me guess, that's not how this works?"

He smirks, and I shake my head, stuffing the mail roughly back into my pocket and flopping down in the nearest chair.

"Coffee?" he offers, not waiting for my response before he starts making me a cup just the way I like it. Maybe he *is* psychic, or maybe he's just really observant. Either way, I desperately need advice, and he's as good an option as anyone.

"Thanks," I say when he sets the steaming cup down at my table and pulls out the chair across from mine to sit down. "You said when you did my palm reading that I have two paths I need to choose from. Did you really not see the right answer, or did you just not want to tell me?"

He leans back in his chair, studying me for several seconds while he drums his long, black fingernails on the table. "I meant it when I said it doesn't work like that. It's not like in the movies where I look at your palm and see a movie in my head about your future. I get feelings and intuitions about things, some stronger than others. That's really it."

I nod in understanding and take a sip from my coffee. "Do you have a gut feeling about what I should do?"

"As a psychic? No. As a friend...why don't we talk it out. Maybe if you say everything out loud, you'll know what the right answer is."

"There was never a question before. This wasn't meant to be forever. I came here to heal after my dad died. I needed a break from life, and the island just sort of called to me, but staying here forever isn't something I considered."

"But you're considering it now?"

I huff out a humorless laugh. "That's crazy, right? Who walks away from a stable future, a future they always wanted, for some guy who's likely to get bored with them in another few weeks anyway?" I stare into the mug of creamy liquid, images of Ten's smile dancing through my mind, the carefree way he laughs, the way he throws himself into everything he does with so much passion and excitement. A smile starts to tug at my lips. "He's sweet though."

"He doesn't strike me as the type to half-ass anything he does. Did he tell you things weren't serious?"

"No." I take another sip from my coffee and finally look up at Raven again. "The first time we…fooled around, he said he didn't know what this was, but it isn't nothing."

"Okay, so why do you think he'll get bored?"

I make another huffy kind of sound and shake my head. "Come on."

"What, come on? I saw the looks you two kept sneaking at each other when we went out to paint the carousel a few days ago."

My stomach flutters and a dopey smile fully overtakes me at the memory of Ten and I chasing each other with paint, kissing when we didn't think anyone was paying attention, not to mention the morning at the beach before that... and that look in his eyes when I told him I didn't think it was such a good idea to spend the night together. My gut twists and my smile falls.

I shift in my seat and feel the crumpled-up letter in my pocket again, which sobers me instantly. "So I should give up everything I planned on for my entire future just because some guy looks at me sweetly?"

"That's the part no one else can decide for you."

I groan and bury my face in my hands.

"Okay." After indulging in a pity party for a few seconds, I straighten myself back up. "I have a couple more months before I have to make a *final* decision, so I can keep enjoying this time with Ten and see what happens later, right?"

"Right," Raven agrees.

"I just can't fall in love with him."

This one is met with a skeptical look from

him. "Right, good luck with that one, babe."

Gah, what does he know anyway? Just because he totally knew that Ten and I were going to get together and Ten is completely perfect and loveable doesn't mean Raven's right about this.

So, fine, I'm already a *little* in love with Ten. I just can't fall any more in love with him. I can handle this.

I hang out with Raven a little longer. Eventually, Hen, Goose, and Lyric come into the shop, the three of them smelling strongly of weed and the beach.

"Excuse me, Mr. Psychic," Hen teases, sauntering over and grabbing a chair to drag to our table. He props his elbows up on the table and smirks at Raven with a look of concentration on his face like he's trying to transmit a telepathic message to him.

"Why, yes, thank you for asking. I *will* make your stoned asses some cookies." Raven pushes his chair back and gets up.

Goose gasps. "Holy shit, he really is psychic."

Raven rolls his eyes, and I chuckle. I'm guessing it didn't take a terrible amount of psychic ability to figure out what they wanted. While he disappears into the kitchen, all three of them join me.

"We just walked past your place, and Ten looks like he's up to something," Lyric tells me with a grin.

"Up to something?"

Goose smacks him on the arm. "It's supposed to be a surprise, dumbass."

"Shit, I forgot. Sorry."

"Wait, what's the surprise?" I lean forward and look between the three of them.

Hen mimes zipping his lips, and the other two just smile at me coyly. "Guess you'll have to go home to find out."

I jump up from my seat. "Raven, how much do I owe you for the coffee?" I call.

He pops his head out from the back. "Don't worry about it."

"That's no way to run a profitable business," Hen teases.

"I was planning on overcharging for the cookies, so I figured I'll still break even."

"Rude," Goose scoffs.

"Still worth it," Lyric says.

I toss a few dollars on the counter anyway and leave the tea shop laughing.

TEN

I'm putting the final touches on the graveyard I've erected in our front yard when Bambi comes up the walk.

"What is all this?" he asks, looking around at the graves, skeleton, and spiderwebs I put up.

"Come on." I hop over a bag of dirt I was using to make realistic-looking fresh graves and grab his hand instead of answering his question. His fingers curl around mine right away, and he laughs as I drag him up the steps and into the house.

I went all out. I wasn't even sure if everything I ordered would get here via the ferry before Halloween, but apparently, miracles do happen.

Bambi gasps as I pull him into the living room, where I did the majority of the decorating. There are spider webs hung up from the corners of the ceiling and various Halloween-themed props covering nearly every surface. I even have the smart speaker playing a spooky playlist to set the mood.

"What is happening?" he asks again, looking around the room with an expression of absolute awe.

"Since you love Halloween, I thought it would be cool to decorate the place for you," I explain with a shrug, my nerves creeping in as I wait for his reaction. Was this too much? Will it make him sad since Halloween was his thing with his dad?

Bambi drops my hand and launches himself into my arms, sending me stumbling when I catch him. I collapse onto the couch with an *oomph*. He peppers my face with enthusiastic kisses that make my heart soar and my cock harden.

"You know that guys who are as hot as you really don't have to try *this* hard, right?" he asks, and I laugh.

"Duly noted. I'll take it all down and stick to just looking good from here on out," I joke.

"No," Bambi gasps. He finally stops kissing me and looks down at me. "Thank you for doing all this."

I wrap my arms around him and hold him to me, trying not to think too hard about the envelope I saw from his med school a few days ago or the fact that he took it with him when he left the house this morning.

"It was fun. Although, I realized when I was almost finished that maybe this is the kind of thing you'd rather have done together. But, hey, next year we can decorate together."

His smile slips. "Yeah, next year."

He stares at me for a few beats, and my heart rate kicks up, the air growing heavy around us. Bambi opens his mouth to say something else—maybe to take back a tentative promise for a faraway future or maybe to say something else entirely, but whatever it is, I'm too afraid to find out.

I kiss him before he can say a word, claiming his lips fiercely. He makes a muffled sound against my mouth as I grab handfuls of his ass. Maybe if I kiss him long enough and hard enough, later doesn't have to come. It can just be the two of us, right here, forever.

I deepen the kiss, a sense of desperation ricocheting through my chest. Bambi seems to be right there with me because he gives as good as he gets, tangling his tongue with mine, tugging at my shirt, not seeming to have any intention of actually getting it off.

My cock swells, pressing against his answering hardness through our clothes. I swallow the gasps and moans Bambi feeds me as we grind on each other, kissing, groping, beyond desperate, beyond lust.

"I want you," he pants, coming up for air between kisses.

"Anything." I thrust against him, getting drunk on the way his eyes roll back and his swollen lips part on another gasp.

"Can I put my mouth on you?" He looks down at me with those wide eyes that make it impossible to deny him anything, and why would I say no to this request anyway?

"Will you let me at least take you to my bedroom this time?" I ask with a grin, and he laughs breathlessly.

"You and your bedroom fetish. Fine, let's go to your bedroom if it will make you feel better."

"Thank you." I grab his ass harder, and he squeaks as I swing my legs around so I'm able to sit up with Bambi straddling me.

I stand in one fluid motion, and he wraps his arms and legs around me like a baby koala, as if I would drop him.

"You're going to hurt yourself," he warns, nibbling on the side of my neck as I carry him down the hallway to my room. There's something so sweet about the fact that he's worried about my back even when we're right in the middle of getting all hot and horny.

"You're light," I counter, and I can feel him smile against my skin.

I crawl onto my bed, and Bambi lets go, looking up at me now as I hover over him. My stomach flips and flutters, my eyes landing on the pretty curve of his lips, damp from my mouth on his.

I go in for another kiss, this one slower and softer, the edgy neediness simmering to something sweeter that I can't quite name. While our lips move together, he slips his hand between us and palms my cock through my shorts, gasping against my lips when my erection throbs in his grip.

I thrust into his palm, groaning from deep in my gut. Each of my piercings rolls and tugs against his hand, sending little ripples of sensation through my shaft, settling in my balls.

"Will you tell me how to do it?" he asks, squeezing a little too hard and then too lightly, kneading my cock as he tries to find just the right stroke. Somehow even his fumbling is the most endearing fucking thing I've ever experienced in my life. He's perfect. He's mine.

The feeling settles in the pit of my stomach, simultaneously comforting and unsettling.

"It's not exactly rocket science," I tease, getting up on my knees and helping him tug my shorts down, my hard cock bouncing free as I shimmy them down and kick them away.

Bambi gives my adorned erection a pointed look, licking his lips. "This isn't a beginner-level situation. What do I do with all of the...?" He runs just the pad of his finger along the row of barbells, and a shiver runs through me.

"Don't overthink it," I advise, my breathing shaky as heat pulses through me, my cock aching and my balls already tightening just from the *thought* of Bambi's lips wrapped around it.

"Okay, but tell me if I mess it up."

"As long as you're involved, there is literally no way you could do it wrong." Maybe I'm overplaying my hand because his eyes widen with the slightest hint of surprise, and he licks his lips again, nodding wordlessly before pushing my chest to get me to lie down on my back.

I crook an arm under my head so I can watch him, spreading my legs comfortably, my cock leaking precum onto my skin as Bambi puts his hands on my thighs and stares down at it like he's trying to solve a puzzle.

My cock jerks and dribbles a little more precum. How is it possible that having him stare at my hard dick is more exciting than most of the blowjobs I've ever gotten?

He drags his finger along the dark, swollen head of my cock, gathering the clear bead of precum and spreading it, his breath hitching right along with mine as I groan and thrust into his not-nearly-enough-touch.

"Bambi," I growl.

"Ryan," he corrects me like he did the other day at the beach, finally wrapping his hand all the way around my cock again.

"Ryan," I moan, humping into his grasp.

He leans forward, his strokes out of rhythm and still not quite the right firmness but fucking perfect for no other reason than the curious, amazed, wide-eyed way he's watching my every reaction, correcting his touch little by little.

The first tentative swipe of his tongue on the underside of my head sends me into orbit, twisting my fingers into my bed sheets, throwing my head back with a low, desperately horny sound.

He does it again, dragging his tongue from the base of my shaft *slowly* up to the head, teasing every one of the barbells mercilessly, making me pant and squirm. When he reaches the head, he doesn't wrap his lips around me like I'm expecting. Instead, he reverses his direction and does it all over again, flicking the tip of his tongue against each piercing one by one. Little ripples of pleasure ricochet through each one, vibrating down my shaft and tightening my balls.

I thrust into his hand, gasping and groaning as he does it again and again, up and down, *up and down.*

"Please," I rasp out when he nears the head of my cock with his mouth for what has to be the millionth time. "Please, fuck, just...*please.*"

My hips twitch helplessly, another wild, desperate sound tearing from my chest as Bambi places a soft, chaste kiss on the head of my cock. Precum trickles out and clings to his lips, and he licks it off with such an innocent fucking expression on his face that it nearly undoes me.

I'm about ready to promise him everything: my house, all the money in my bank account, my undying devotion, *anything* if he'll just fucking put my cock in his mouth already. My thigh muscles tense and my toes curl, my hips moving all on their own, my erection bumping helplessly against his chin.

"Wow," he murmurs, holding the base of my cock in a firm grip and brushing the head of my cock back and forth against his mouth. "I didn't know how...*powerful* it would feel to do this."

He strokes me slowly again, his hold just right now, firm and more confident, his hot breath fanning over my head.

Finally, *finally,* he wraps his lips around me. A hoarse cry tears from my throat, my whole body trembling with the effort of holding back the urge to force my cock deep into his throat, fucking his mouth to chase the orgasm he built inside me with all of his teasing.

Like his grip, the first touch of his mouth is tentative and unsure. He sucks experimentally on my crown, flicking his tongue back and forth, sending sparks through me. I clench and unclench my fingers from the sheets, writhing under his touch as he slowly takes me just a little deeper, testing the fullness of my cock inside his mouth with every inch. When the first barbell passes his lips, he rolls his tongue across it, bobbing his head and sucking at the same time.

Bambi's muffled little moaning noises accompany the wet, sloppy sound of his mouth on me and my half-insane pants and pleas echoing around the humid bedroom.

He takes more of me slowly, so fucking slowly, until I hit the fleshy back of his throat. He gags, his throat and tongue all tightening around my cock at once, a few stray tears streaking down his cheeks. I jackknife off the bed, pleasure spiking through me, white-hot and fucking electric.

I grit my teeth and grapple to get my body under control. "You okay?" I manage to grit out as Bambi goes back to taking just the head of my cock into his mouth. He nods without releasing me, humming to assure me he's fine. The sound vibrates down my shaft. "Here."

I grab his hand and put it back on my cock, my hand over his to show him he can stroke me at the same time so he doesn't have to try to take me so deep. He hums again, starting to get the hang of it, his head moving up and down along with his hand. My length is soaked with his spit already, so his hand moves easily over me, every stroke tugging at my piercings and making my balls pull tighter, my impending orgasm getting more and more impatient.

"I'm so close," I warn in a strained voice.

He makes another sound and sucks me faster, taking me a little deeper again, but more carefully this time. He falls into the perfect rhythm, every pass of his mouth and hand over me pushing me closer and closer to the edge.

My thighs start to tremble again, the heat in the pit of my stomach creeping through me, my heart hammering so wildly I can hear my pulse thundering in my ears. I manage to untangle my fingers from the sheets and push against his head in warning. He takes me harder, faster, making desperate, hungry noises like the only thing he's ever wanted in life is a mouth full of my cum.

"Ryan," I gasp his name again and lose the

battle with my self-control. My balls constrict and my toes curl, my fingers grasping at his hair as I pump hot, sticky ropes of cum onto his tongue.

He releases me a few seconds too soon, the last few shots of my release panting his chin and cheeks. Bambi looks up at me, his eyes clouded with lust, his cheeks pink, completely debauched by me. He's trembling, and for a second, I'm worried I might have hurt him, pulled his hair too hard, or maybe lost control without realizing it and forced myself too deep while I was coming.

He scrambles onto his knees and shoves his shorts down frantically. His cock is dark with arousal and so fucking hard. He wraps his hand around himself, throwing his head back and crying out after only a couple of strokes, covering my thighs and now-soft cock with his cum.

I haven't even had the chance to catch my breath from my orgasm before he's crawling up next to me and collapsing. I manage to wrap my arms around him and tug him to me while we both drag in ragged breaths.

Eventually, our breathing evens out, and he gets more comfortable, draping himself half over me, neither of us seeming all that concerned with the sweat and cum getting smeared between us.

"Hey, how did I get stuck with the nickname Bambi anyway?" he asks in a grumbly tone. "I mean, I know I'm a bit gangly, but I didn't think I was baby deer gangly."

I chuckle. "It's your devastatingly sweet doe eyes," I inform him, brushing a kiss to his forehead and smiling against his skin. His hair is damp with sweat, and his skin exudes the scent of the beach and sex. I groan softly, my dick making an attempt to harden again.

"Huh," he hums. "How'd you end up with the name Ten?"

"My full name is Tennyson," I confess.

"It is?" He pulls back and looks at me with surprise and amusement.

I nod. "What, did you think it was because I had a ten-inch dick?"

Bambi wrinkles his nose and blushes a little. "No."

"Liar. You thought I was packing a solid ten inches and were totally disappointed by my modest seven-inch cock," I tease, feigning offense.

He cackles. "I might have wondered about it once or twice, but I am far from disappointed and *modest* is the last word I would use to describe any part of you, let alone your cock."

I tilt his face up and press more soft, sweet

kisses to his lips, savoring the taste of him and the boneless, relaxed feeling of him in my arms.

"Hey, Tennyson?" he asks when we break the kiss.

I grin. "Yeah, Ryan?"

"What are we doing?" There's a vulnerability in his voice as he cuddles closer, tucking his head into the crook of my neck. To avoid looking at me or just to be close?

My heart beats wildly. What are we doing? I don't know about him, but I think I'm falling in love.

Fuck.

That thought hits me like a ton of bricks.

It's hard to pinpoint *one* moment where I went from intrigued by Bambi to head over heels in love with him, but I think that's because there wasn't a single moment. I think I've been slowly falling in love with him from the minute he showed up at The Sand Bar two years ago.

The words rise to the tip of my tongue, but I bite them back. That envelope came from his med school, and it doesn't take a genius to figure out what's likely inside. He still needs to decide whether he's staying, and I'm not sure if hiding away on an island—even a paradise like this one—is what's going to make him happy forever. Even if I'm desperate to keep him right here with me.

I brush my fingers through his hair and kiss the top of his head.

"I don't know," I lie. "It's beautiful, though, isn't it?"

He pulls back just enough to look up at me. "I didn't know you were such a romantic." He smiles, his eyes soft around the edges, his body heavy and relaxed against mine.

"Don't tell anybody. It would ruin my reputation," I joke, and he mimes zipping his lips.

"Your secret is safe with me."

CHAPTER 20

BAMBI

"So what's today's adventure?" I can't believe I'm asking that. If my dad could see me now, not only willingly stepping away from movies and studying but actively excited to go out and do something physical, he wouldn't believe it.

Ten grins, leaning on the kitchen counter with a mug of coffee in his outstretched hand. If there's a more beautiful sight in the world than that, I don't want to know about it.

"We're going to the waterfall," he says, and I narrow my eyes at him.

"I'm not convinced the waterfall even exists," I tease.

"It exists. And if it doesn't, consider it a nice morning on the mountain."

"Fine, but I'm not carrying any paint," I bargain.

"Deal," he agrees with a laugh.

I cross the kitchen, taking the mug from

him. I don't take a sip from it though. Instead, I set it on the counter and step into his arms, tilting my head back to grin at him.

"Good morning."

Ten rests his forehead against mine, our smiles matching. "Morning, Bambi. You know, it's kind of silly for you to keep sleeping all the way down the hall when my bed is plenty big enough for two."

It's the first time he's brought it up since I turned him down the other night, but he's lingered in the hallway each night, clearly wanting to ask me again.

It sounds nice to go to sleep next to him, to wake up next to him, to spend all night with his body wrapped all around mine. It sounds way better than nice, actually. But I'm afraid if I get used to something like that, it'll be over, and I'll never leave.

Ten brushes a kiss to my forehead, and my stomach flutters.

Maybe I won't leave anyway.

"I told you, I kick a lot in my sleep," I lie. I can tell by his expression that he's not buying it, but he doesn't argue.

"Say the word, and I'll buy shin guards. But until then, we hike," he declares, wrapping his arms around me and spinning us around until

I'm throwing my head back and laughing. When the world stops twirling, his mouth lands on mine, and I get dizzy all over again.

It's a little past noon by the time we've managed to stop kissing, have coffee and breakfast, and leave the house.

It's a little cooler today, with October more than halfway over now. If you would've told me a few years ago during a negative ten-degree New York winter that I would ever consider fifty-five degrees cool, I would've laughed, but my body has already adjusted to the island weather. It's hard to imagine going back now. Can I?

I look at Ten just a few paces ahead of me, stopping to hold a tree branch out of the way so I can pass without getting hit in the face with it. I'm really not sure I can go back anyway. Anxiety has become a constant for me lately, twisting in my gut at yet another reminder that the deadline is looming. I have to decide soon, and I've never been more torn.

"Hey, look," Ten says, drawing my attention up ahead a bit. There's a large tree just off the main path. I can't tell what it is about it that's drawing his attention at first, but as we get closer, I notice hundreds of initials carved into the trunk along with little hearts and a few other simple messages and dates.

"This is so cool." I reach out to run my

fingers along a few of the rough groves, coded names of men who have stopped here for years and years, immortalizing a moment in time they didn't want to let pass them by.

"I think that's what makes this island so special. There are ghosts of all the love that's been found. It stays in the air and in the ocean and in the sand." He touches the tree too. "And in the trees, apparently."

"I don't think most of it is love," I argue, thinking of all of the drunken, wild, vacation flings that we see night after night at the bar, men who may think they're infatuated for one night but will forget the other's name by the time they get home.

Ten looks in my direction, our eyes meeting and lingering, something heavy passing between us.

"Some of it is love," he says, and my heart does a flip.

All I can do is blink at him, trying and failing to find words to say back. Is he saying he's falling in love with me?

He reaches into his pocket and pulls out a pocketknife. "Let's add ours," he suggests, and I nod dumbly, still unable to find my voice as my world rearranges itself. Ten might love me?

He carves our initials, using an "R" for

mine instead of the "B" for Bambi. I smile like a fool as he adds today's date and a lopsided, messy heart.

When he's done, I reach out to trace it with my fingers. "Ten, I..." I'm not sure what I'm planning to say, and thankfully he saves me from having to try to figure it out, cutting me off with a quick kiss and another smile.

"Come on, I can hear the waterfall."

TEN

I've been to the waterfall a handful of times, usually with Easy, Trick, and Lux, but a couple times with tourists during brief flings. It's nice. There's a romantic vibe, and I dig it. But seeing Bambi's eyes go wide as he kicks off his shoes and rushes over to dip his feet in the water, hearing his giddy laughter at the light spray hitting his skin, watching him tilt his head back to catch the sun shining through the trees…this might just be my new favorite place in the whole world.

Scratch that. My favorite place is wherever Bambi is.

I take my shoes off and join him by the little pond made by the waterfall, sitting down on the grassy edge and dipping my feet in next to his.

We sit together quietly for a while, swinging our feet in the cold water, listening to the birds in the trees above us. His hand brushes against mine in the grass, and I hook my pinky around his, a sense of contentment settling into my chest.

Maybe if he decides to leave, I can go with him. Would he agree to visit the island from time to time? The thought of not being able to wake up and take my board straight to the ocean weighs heavy on my chest but not heavier than the idea of watching Bambi walk away.

"I think Raven's costume party is this weekend," Bambi says, bringing my thoughts back to the island for the time being.

"It is. I wasn't sure you'd want to go."

"Are you kidding? I never miss a chance to go to a costume party."

I don't point out that he skipped it the last two years running. "You have a costume in mind? We're going to match, right?"

His cheeks turn the slightest shade of pink. "I might have a few ideas."

"Lay 'em on me," I prompt.

"How do we feel about gender-bending?" he asks.

"Pro. But I should warn you, I look hella

sexy with a pair of fake tits, so you're going to have to brace yourself."

He throws his head back and laughs. "Consider me warned."

We spend the rest of the early afternoon trading increasingly silly costume suggestions and making out in the grass. By the time we start back to town, the sun is getting lower in the sky and our stomachs are rumbling.

"Do you smell that?" Bambi asks, sticking his nose in the air and sniffing as we walk hand in hand down the main street. "It smells amazing."

My stomach grumbles again and my mouth waters. It smells like dinner is what it smells like. We pass the restaurant right next to The Sand Bar, Storm's restaurant, and surprisingly, the lights are all on.

I slow my steps to look in through the window and find what looks to be half the town inside, filling all the tables.

"Let's see what's up," I suggest.

"There you guys are. We were considering sending out a search party," Trick says when we step inside.

"We must have missed our invitation. What's going on?" I ask.

"There was a text chain. I sent you one," Easy says. "Storm *claims* he has ingredients that are about to go bad, and he doesn't want to waste them. I think he's just fucking bored without any tourists here to cook for. Either way, free food."

"Free food from *Storm*," Lux adds, and several people nod in reverent agreement.

"Count us in." Bambi points out a couple of empty chairs, and we go to grab them, pulling them over while the guys make room at the table.

It's noisy and hectic inside the restaurant with so many people crowded inside, but the food smells incredible, and it looks even better once Hen starts bringing it out, complaining about having to work in October like a normal person. I pull some cash out of my pocket and stuff it into his jeans, and everyone else follows suit until he looks like a stripper with bills sticking out of his waistband and all of his pockets.

Bambi is pulled from one conversation to another, first with Trick, then with Raven, next with Goose. For a guy who swore he didn't have any friends or liked socializing only a couple of months ago, he's certainly come out of his shell.

I can't stop watching him, turning over the idea of following him if he decides to leave. Can I? Should I? I swore I would die on this island before I'd leave, but he could be worth it.

"Why are you looking at me like that?" he asks, wiping at his face like there must be food there.

"Like what?" I tease, bumping my foot against his under the table.

"Weirdo." He smiles and shakes his head at me, and I lean over to kiss him.

I don't know if I can leave the island without leaving a big part of myself behind, but I do know that I can't watch him go without me.

CHAPTER 21

TEN

I can hear the music and see the flames of Raven's giant bonfire illuminating the night sky from a block away. I use my grip on Bambi's hand to tug him even closer to me so I can throw my arm around him, loving the way his smaller body fits perfectly against mine. After much debate, we settled on our costumes and managed to put them together in time.

The fur from Bambi's wolf ears tickles me, and when he looks up, all fucking cute with whiskers and a black nose painted on his face, I can't stop myself from leaning down to kiss him, my red hood falling over my face in the process.

He giggles and kisses me back and then pushes on my chest. "You're going to smear my makeup before anyone even sees it."

"Not sorry." I flash him an unrepentant smirk and then steer him around the back of Raven's house as we reach it. There's a sidewalk that leads to his boardwalk, which goes straight down to the beach, where the party is already getting underway.

"Does anyone throw an indoor party around here?" Bambi muses, and I scoff.

"Who in their right mind would be inside when the beach is *right* here?" I wave at the ocean.

"I guess that's fair."

I lean down and nip at the side of his jaw because it's there, and I'm so fucking wild about him I can't stop touching him. Never once in my thirty-six years of life did I wonder if I was missing out on anything by being relationship-averse, but now I think I was just waiting for Bambi without ever realizing it.

I look over to Easy and Trick, who, along with Lux, are dressed in skin-tight black body suits, all wearing cat ears. They give me a thumbs-up to let me know they set up the surprise I asked for help with. I mouth *thank you* and then sweep Bambi into my arms to sway to the music for a minute.

He laughs, following my lead and dancing clumsily to the atmospheric music Raven has playing through a few portable speakers.

"You two are adorable," Raven says, approaching us with a couple of cups of what looks like cider. He's dressed in a black and gold corset that he's absolutely rocking the hell out of, his face heavily made up with black eye makeup and bright-red lipstick. He looks gorgeous, but in my opinion, he's got absolutely nothing on my man.

"Thank you." Bambi takes the cups and passes one to me.

Just like every year, Raven has gone all out for this party. There's a barrel of apples to bob for, pumpkins to carve, a table with tarot cards laid out as well as a Ouija board. That's not even mentioning all of the snacks and drinks.

"Mind if I steal your little wolf for a few?" Raven asks.

I let go of Bambi. "Just don't let him wander into the ocean," I warn.

Bambi rolls his eyes and groans. "Am I *ever* going to live that down?"

"It only happened two months ago," I point out. Damn, was it really that recent? It simultaneously feels like yesterday and a lifetime ago since he came to live with me and changed everything.

I join my friends, who are in the middle of a discussion about whether or not it's actually possible to give a blowjob underwater or if you'll drown trying. This is the quality content I stick around for.

Every so often, I glance over at Bambi to find him laughing with Raven, Hen, Goose, and Lyric. It looks like they're conspiring about something, but I couldn't begin to guess what. He looks over—maybe feeling my eyes on him or just drawn to me the same way I am to him— and our gazes meet from across the party, lingering for several seconds.

"You're such a fucking sap," Trick bumps me with his shoulder.

"Jealous," I taunt, shooting Bambi a wink and then returning my attention to my friends.

"Yeah, actually, I am," he confesses.

I raise my eyebrows at him, shocked by his admission. I know he has a thing for Boston, but in all honesty, I always figured it was more rooted in the fact that Boston is the one man who's resisted all of his advances since the moment they both arrived on Palm Island.

He takes a swig from his cup and laughs. "Actually, I think I'm just drunk. Don't listen to any of the bullshit I'm spouting."

Easy claps him on the back. "We never do," he assures him, and we all laugh.

Eventually, Bambi drags his friends over to join our little group, and we all enjoy the party together. Hen even manages to keep the death glares at Easy to a bare minimum.

"We have the best costumes," Bambi whispers to me as we gather around Raven's table to get our tarot cards read by him.

He's not wrong. Angel and Devil dressed predictably as an Angel and a Devil. *Yawn.* Boston looks pretty hot, dressed like a lumber jack, an axe over his shoulder, his plaid shirt only half-buttoned, exposing his hairy chest. Trick is clearly a fan, casting glances at him whenever he doesn't think the other man is looking. Goose and Hennessey are dressed in grass skirts and coconut bras. And Lyric is wearing the same clothes he always wears. Whether he didn't feel like bothering with a costume or forgot that it was Halloween, the world may never know.

"We do," I agree, kissing him again because I can't get enough of the taste of his lips.

Hennessey gets his cards read first, a knowing little smirk on Raven's lips the whole time he shuffles and pulls the cards. "A storm is coming," he says, and Hen rolls his eyes.

"It's hurricane season," he points out in a bored tone. "You're going to have to do better than that."

"Hm, interesting," Raven hums. "I see dishonesty and sex."

"Yeah, the two tend to go hand in hand," Hen quips.

Raven glares at him. "Your negative energy really isn't helping, babe."

He sighs. "Fine, I'll be good."

"Thank you." Raven studies the cards a little longer and then looks at him again. "You're ready to put the past behind you and move on."

"What past?"

"That's it, that's what I see," he answers vaguely, shrugging and then gathering the cards back up to reshuffle.

"Do me?" Angel asks, sauntering forward, his blond curls framing his face as he looks Raven over with an unexpectedly intense gaze.

Raven's hands tremble, sending his cards flying in all directions. He licks his lips and scrambles to gather them back up. It almost seems like he's purposefully avoiding looking at Angel. Devil joins his husband, kissing his cheek and putting an arm around his shoulders.

"Yeah, do a reading for us," he echoes.

"I see the two of you living happily ever after. Okay, who's next?" He hurriedly casts his eyes around the rest of the group while Devil and Angel exchange wordless looks that are impossible to interpret. Raven's eyes land on the two of us. "What about you, Bambi? Do you want to see what the cards have to say?"

I expect him to jump at the chance, if only for the novelty of it, but he shakes his head quickly. "I'm not sure I'm ready to know anything right now."

I squeeze his hand, my chest constricting at the same time. He's not ready to know because he thinks it's going to suggest he should leave. Does that mean that's what he *wants*? I resist the urge to wrap my arms around him and beg him not to go. Instead, I tug his hand a little, my plan for the rest of tonight suddenly feeling absolutely perfect.

"Come on, I've got a surprise for you," I whisper near his ear, pulling him away from the party and down the beach.

BAMBI

I stumble down the beach after Ten, feeling light and giddy and just a little bit scandalous after what Lyric slipped into my pocket earlier. I don't know what Ten has planned, but I'm sure whatever it is will be an adventure. Everything with him always is.

My heart trips and I squeeze his hand tighter.

"We're almost there," he says, and I can see something illuminated a little farther down the beach. I just can't tell what it is.

As we get closer, the whole setting comes

into view, and my breath catches.

"I can't believe you did this. It's so fucking sappy," I sniff, looking at the blankets laid out, surrounded by colorful Christmas lights, pillows piled around the edges to make it the perfect place to lie down and look up at the stars... among other things.

"You like it?" he checks.

I grab his shirt and drag him in for a kiss, pushing up on my toes to close the distance and devour his lips. He grabs my ass to lift me up, and I wrap my legs around his waist, sliding my tongue over his inside the heat of his mouth. He stumbles a few steps and then trips, the two of us crashing onto the makeshift bed under the stars.

I laugh, his chest rumbling with amusement against mine. He braces himself, pushing up out of the reach of my mouth.

"I have something," I tell him with a teasing smirk.

"Yeah, me too," he jokes, rolling his hips so I can feel the hard length of his arousal.

I moan and then chuckle, wiggling around to get to my pocket and pulling out the little gummy edible that Lyric gave me. I thought about giving it back, but then Hen and Goose had started going on and on about how amazing sex feels when you're stoned, and I got curious enough to hang on to it.

"Is that what I think it is?" Ten asks, raising his eyebrows at me. I nod. "Do I need to remind you what happened last time?"

"I remember, but I figure one more time won't hurt. I promise not to wander into the ocean," I vow. "Besides, I'm told that stoned sex is next level."

He gives a rough chuckle. "If the sex between us gets any better, it might kill us."

"It's a risk I'm willing to take. It'll be fun. We don't even have to have sex. I was just kidding. It would be cool to get stoned and look at the stars for a few hours. It would be a much better way for you to remember me," I joke lightly, wishing I could call the words back as soon as they slip out. I haven't decided yet, not really, but it's been on my mind. Ten's eyes darken.

"All right." He rolls onto the cushion next to me and props one arm behind his head. "Let's do it."

I put it between my teeth, the distinct flavor meeting my lips immediately, the marijuana mixed with just a hint of sugary sweetness. His eyes are full of heat and amusement, but there's an undercurrent of something more serious. Is he thinking about the same thing I am? Is he hoping I stay? Should I? I bite the gummy in half and Ten parts his lips so I can pop the remaining bit into his mouth.

I chew it slowly and then swallow, making a choice to let go of all of my worries about the future. That's tomorrow's problem. Tonight is just about this moment.

"I don't feel anything," I say with a frown when nothing immediately happens.

Ten laughs. "Come here." He gestures for me to lie down next to him. "Edibles take a while to kick in. Let's just look at the stars until then."

So that's what we do, look up at the stars and talk about things that aren't scary or too big, letting the sound of the waves and the vastness of the sky overhead pull us into the illusion that we're the only people in the world, and this is the only moment that exists.

Slowly, *very* slowly, the feeling of being stoned creeps over me. I know there are all kinds of weed, and it's obvious this one feels different from before. I don't feel floaty or giggly. I feel... heavy, relaxed, *horny*.

I glance over at Ten, the dim light from the Christmas lights illuminating his features.

Or maybe it's the company rather than the weed making this time feel so different.

I snuggle close to Ten, laying my head on his chest and looking up at the immense sky overhead, a blanket of the deepest blue as far as the eye can see, stars shining from one end to the other.

"Wow," I sigh.

"Very," Ten agrees, lazily dragging his fingers through my hair. The slow stroking tempts my eyes to close, but I don't want to waste a second of this moment.

My body buzzes with slow, pulsing energy. I'm vaguely aware that my cock is hard…actually, *achingly* hard when I let myself think about it…but even that feels lazy, as if we have all the time in the world to get to it.

I tilt my head back so our faces are a few inches apart. Ten's lips curl with a slow smile, his eyelids drooping. Our noses bump, and my stomach flutters violently as if this was our first kiss.

But when his lips meet mine, it's so much better than a first. This kiss is made of all the memories we've shared in the last two months. It's exciting and familiar all at once. He knows how I like to be kissed now, and so do I. I'm no longer the fumbling, awkward virgin I was when I got a nosebleed all over him, at least not with Ten. There's still plenty more for me to experience with him, but none of it is scary anymore because I know he'll take care of me.

His tongue moves against mine, syrupy

slow and addictive as hell.

I wonder if Ten would come with me if I asked him to. Would it be fair to even find out? Taking Ten off the island is like snatching a tiger out of the jungle and putting it in a cage. I know I shouldn't, but I'm not sure I'm selfless enough to keep myself from doing it.

"This is my favorite moment ever," I murmur into his mouth, and Ten smiles. "I think I'm in love with you." My throat tightens as soon as the words are out. What if he doesn't feel the same way? Am I breaking the rules of whatever this is?

He catches my lips with his, the kiss hard and over too soon. "I'm really glad it's not just me." Ten tightens an arm around me, tugging me closer. "I'm in love with you too. I'm so fucking in love with you."

Our mouths find each other again, my hard cock pressed to his thigh. The floaty feeling starts to kick in, but it's still different, more tethered than last time. Every inch of my body tingles and pulses, the barest brush of Ten's fingers on my skin making me gasp and squirm. The night is cool enough that the heat of his body feels incredible when I plaster myself against him, climbing onto his lap to straddle him.

My cock throbs and pulses, trapped in my briefs. I can feel the shape of his arousal through his pants. Ten drags his hands all over my body like he's trying to memorize every inch of me.

I hump against him, reaching to unbutton my pants with one hand, my other arm trembling with the full weight of my body. Ten gets his pants open, exposing his thick, hot cock. The ladder of barbells down the length of his cock rolls against me as I thrust into him again with my pants around my thighs.

The cushions shift around us, and we sink deeper into the pile. Ten's laughter is muffled by my mouth, his cock jerking and flexing with the sound. I chuckle and moan around his tongue. Shockwaves spark through me, my head dragging over his with every thrust. Each touch of his mouth against mine feels like an individual orgasm.

Ten tangles his fingers through my hair and kisses me deeper, grunting and moaning into my mouth as he fucks it with his tongue. I brace my hands on his chest, my fingers finding their way to his taut nipples. Another moan vibrates down my tongue as I tease him with my thumbs and then pinch both nipples.

He hisses and arches toward me, his cock twitching again, spilling slick, sticky precum over my shaft. Ten fucks his cock against mine, the texture of his piercings sending jolts through me, settling in my balls and tightening them.

"Tennyson," I groan his name, and I can feel the curve of his smile against my lips.

"Ryan," he murmurs, nipping at my bottom lip.

The sound of my name on his lips sends me over the edge. I gasp and pant, my cock spasming as I spill thick ropes of my release all over him. Ten's hands find my ass, digging into my cheeks and holding me to him as he thrusts harder and faster, his cock gliding through the mess I've made with my cum.

He curses and shudders, the throbbing of his orgasm dragging out my own. Even once we're both spent, we continue to thrust lazily against each other, our kisses as slow and sweet as honey.

Eventually, I roll off him, our mixed cum already drying in my pubes. We can shower off in the beach showers before we walk home, but right now, I just want to lie here with him. Ten seems to be in agreement, sighing peacefully and tucking me under his arm so we can both watch the stars a while longer.

Walking home in the middle of the night, sticky with cum and still thoroughly stoned, is a blur. Did we clean up our blankets? Were we supposed to? I guess we can always get them tomorrow.

Ten keeps an arm around me, anchoring me close as we stumble into the house.

We reach his bedroom door, and I try to keep walking down the hall, instinctively heading for my room, but he tightens his arm to stop me.

"Come sleep with me," he pleads right next to my ear, his breath warm and his body even warmer. Did he leave his red hooded cape back at the beach? And where's my wolf hood?

"I—"

He cuts me off with a hard kiss. "Please?" he begs again, and I crack.

I told him I love him, he loves me back. Not sleeping in his bed isn't going to make this choice any easier at this point.

Love is supposed to conquer all, isn't it? Maybe we can find a way to make this work. Harry wouldn't leave us hanging, would he? That's what Ten believes: soul mates, true love, all that stuff I used to think was silly. Maybe I was just afraid it was for everyone but me.

I nod, bumping my nose against his and letting him drag me into his room. We strip out of the clothes we managed to wear back to the house and tumble into his bed together.

"Come on, I like to be the little spoon,"

he says, rolling onto his side and then groping blindly to drag me close. I throw a leg over his hips and wrap my arms around him.

"I feel like more of a jetpack than a spoon," I mutter sleepily, the hazy fog from the weed making his bed feel ridiculously comfortable. Or maybe it's just that Ten is here.

"Jetpack me, baby," he jokes, and we both laugh, his body moving against mine in a way I vow to remember for the rest of my life, no matter what happens later.

We'll figure it out. We have to.

CHAPTER 22

TEN

I wake up with Bambi's smaller body still draped all around me. His skin is sticky with sweat and so is mine. I'm also very aware of the dried cum crusted on my stomach and pubes. Gross, but ten out of ten, would do again.

I smile sleepily and thread my fingers through his to keep his arm nice and snug around me, playing back the hazy memories from last night: the beach, the sex, Bambi telling me he loves me.

My body goes hot and cold at the same time, leaving me feeling clammy and unsettled. Bambi's in love with me. Did he mean it, or was it the weed and the romantic setting talking? And what does this mean as far as what comes next?

What if he decides against finishing med school just because of me? Can I live with that?

He stirs behind me, tightening his grip around me and yawning loudly.

"Oh my god, your bed is amazing," he

mumbles.

"Don't you wish you'd agreed to sleep here sooner?" I tease, easing his hold on me and rolling to face him. I grab his calf to keep his leg hitched over me, and I wrap my arms around his body to pull him close.

The warmth of his bare body and the feeling of him in my arms has my cock hard in an instant.

I drag my fingers through his hair, making it even messier than sleep managed. He has an adorably sleepy smile stretched over his lips, his eyes only half-open but fixed on me all the same, like there's nothing else in the world that has any right to his attention. Fuck, I like that. I like everything about him, every inch of him.

We meet in a slow, lazy kiss. Bambi puts his palm to my chest, no doubt feeling how hard my heart is pounding for him.

"I want you inside me," he whispers, dragging a low groan from me. "I want everything with you. I'm so in love with you."

I kiss his chin, his nose, his cheeks, wanting my lips on every inch I can reach, my heart going wild at his fully sober admission. "I love you so damn much. I don't know how I looked at you every day for two years and didn't see it sooner. I must be a fucking idiot."

My next kiss lands right back on his mouth, cutting off his peel of laughter and turning it into a moan as I roll my hips to drag my hot, hard cock against his.

"Will you fill me up and make me yours?" Bambi pants, flicking his tongue along my bottom lip and curling his fingers on my chest.

"You're already mine." I reluctantly unwrap one arm from around him so I can blindly grope for the supplies I need in the bedside drawer.

He spots the condom in my hand and bites his lip. "Do we, um, have to?"

"What? Use a condom?"

Bambi nods. "I want to feel you. I want your cum dripping out of me later. I want you to mark me inside. Please?"

Heat rushes over my skin as my cock throbs. Fuck, I want that.

"Are you sure? You know I wasn't exactly a saint before we got together. I'm on PrEP, and I get tested every six months or so, but…"

"Please?" he says again.

I toss the condom aside and fumble to get the lube open, squirting a generous amount onto my fingers before pulling Bambi close to me again.

I slip my slicked fingers between his cheeks in search of his hole. When my fingertips graze his tight, puckered entrance, he gasps into my mouth, his cock jerking against mine.

"So sweet and tight," I murmur, nuzzling his nose with mine as I gently tease his rim, slowly coaxing him to relax, waking up all of the nerve endings he doesn't even know he has.

He whimpers and whines, his hips twitching impatiently, but I'm not about to rush any part of this. There's only one first time. Of course, there will also be his first second time, his first third time, his first fourth time…and I intend to have every one of them.

"Have you ever had anything inside of you?" I ask, testing the softness of his hole by pressing my index finger just a little harder to his pucker.

His breath is coming in sweet little pants, puffing over my face as he shakes his head quickly, his cheeks going that pretty shade of pink I love so much.

"Not even your own fingers?" I nip at his chin. He shakes his head again, and his hole slowly gives way to the tip of my finger. He's so unbelievably tight and scorching hot inside. My cock aches, dribbling precum in anticipation of being inside the vice grip he calls an ass.

I work my finger inside of him so incredibly slow that I'm impressed with my restraint. His inner muscles relax for me an inch at a time, sucking me in deeper and deeper until I'm up to my last knuckle, my free fingers brushing his balls.

Bambi breathes heavily, still thrusting against me in little jerks, his skin flushed and his whole body trembling.

"I can't get enough of you." I slip my tongue between his lips and press my finger just a little deeper, wiggling it inside him until he starts to hump into me more desperately. "I'm fucking wild about you, Ryan."

He cries out, digging his fingers into my biceps hard enough that it will likely leave a bruise later. I want more. I want everyone to look at me and know that I belong to Bambi just as much as he belongs to me.

"More," he gasps. "Please, more. Please, please."

I pull my finger out and gently thrust it back inside a few times, ignoring his impatience. He'll get more, but not before I'm ready. I claim his lips again, getting drunk on the taste of his muffled, pleasured sounds as they vibrate over my tongue while I take my time fingering him open.

When I'm ready, I blindly drizzle more lube onto my fingers and add a second. He bucks and moans, his cock jerking so violently I'm surprised he manages to hold his orgasm back. It's fucking addictive. Would it be a reasonable life goal to just spend every waking second with my fingers buried inside his hole, making him shake and beg for me?

By the time I'm satisfied with how soft and open his hole is, my balls are heavy and aching, my cock hard and slicked with the precum that's been drooling from my slit for fuck knows how long now.

Bambi makes a noise of protest as I ease my fingers out of him and roll his boneless body over so he's the little spoon now.

"I got you, baby," I promise, nipping at his earlobe while I coat my cock with even more lube and get myself into position.

When he feels the head of my erection nudge his hole, he goes still, holding his breath.

"Deep breath and try to relax for me," I say, kissing along the side of his neck to relax him and circling his rim with my cock the same way I did with my fingers.

He pulls in a sharp breath and then another, a few more, and he finally starts to relax again, his pucker loosening a little. I bury my nose in the crook of his neck, breathing in deeply, filling my lungs with everything that is Bambi.

We both gasp when I breach the tight ring of muscles and ease my way inside of him. I fill him with my cock a fraction of an inch at a time, being extra careful as each one of the barbells in my shaft tugs against his rim before slipping inside. By the time I'm buried fully inside of him, we're both breathing heavily, beads of sweat forming on our skin.

I wrap both my arms around him and put one hand on his chest so I can feel his heartbeat. I stay like that for a minute, my cock throbbing inside the tight grip of his ass, our bodies pressed so fully against each other it's hard to tell where I end, and he begins.

"Tennyson," he rasps my name, turning his head to the side so he can see me.

I claim his lips the best I can from this angle, moving inside him with shallow thrusts, not willing to pull out more than an inch before filling him again, my hips flush to his ass, our bodies entwined.

His tongue brushes over mine, our kisses growing messier and clumsier as we both become more desperate, groaning and panting, trembling and gasping, fucking aching for each other even though we couldn't possibly have any more than we do right now.

Bambi gasps into my mouth, and that's the only warning I have before his inner muscles constrict around me so tightly that I see stars. He starts to pulse around me, crying out as his orgasm overtakes him, the throbbing waves of it rippling around my cock until my thrusts stutter and I follow him over the edge.

I flood him with my cum, forcing my cock as deep as possible as I pump hot ropes of my release inside him. My orgasm feels like it goes on forever, spurred on by his, the two of us moving together, chasing every last aftershock until we're both completely spent and out of breath. Even then, I try to keep my softening cock inside of him as long as I can, not wanting to lose the feeling of connection I've found buried deep in Bambi.

When I finally slip free, I press my nose to his sweaty hair and kiss his head.

"I love you," he murmurs again, his voice ragged and sounding just on the edge of sleep, or maybe more of a sex coma.

"I love you," I echo, kissing him a few more times as his breathing slows.

I love his sweetness and the fact that he can sit through every manner of terrifying movie without so much as flinching. I love that he's happy as can be sitting at home, enjoying his own company, but is just as willing to go along for any adventure I can come up with. But more than anything, I love that he has big dreams, and the last thing I want to do is steal those from him.

I just wish I could know what that will end up meaning.

I lie next to him for a while, trailing my fingers up and down the curve of his spine and listening to the slow, even rhythm of his breath.

My phone vibrates on my nightstand, and I roll over to grab it, to keep the sound from waking Bambi, if nothing else. There's a text from Easy waiting in the group thread. It's a picture of donuts and the caption: *Fresh out of the oven. For eating, not for dick measuring.* I chuckle quietly and consider just closing out of the thread without responding. But when I look over at Bambi's sleeping form again, all of the doubts about the future rush over me again.

TEN: Be there in a few. Make some coffee.

EASY: Would a please kill you?

TEN: It might.

TRICK: Seconding the coffee, and I refuse to beg.

EASY: Ungrateful heathens.

I laugh again and slip out of bed, careful not to wake Bambi.

I take a lightning-fast shower and get dressed quickly, and I'm walking into Easy's house less than fifteen minutes later, not bothering to knock. The smell of sugary donuts has my stomach rumbling and my mouth watering instantly.

"Long night?" Easy asks as soon as I step into the kitchen. He and Lux are at the table, and there's a full pot of coffee on the counter right next to the rack of fresh donuts.

I smirk at him. "Gloriously so. Thanks again for setting up that romantic beach thing for me."

"You know you can always count on your wingmen."

His words hit me square in the chest. When I've considered leaving the island with Bambi, I've thought about how much it will suck to miss out on the surfing and the hiking. I haven't let myself think about leaving my best friends behind.

"What was that look?" he asks.

I ignore his question for a second, focusing my attention on pouring a cup of coffee and grabbing a donut while I work out my thoughts.

When I finally do, I turn around and lean on the counter, looking right at Lux. "Was it hard leaving your whole life behind to follow Easy out here?"

His forehead wrinkles as he frowns. "I didn't really think about it. What was my alternative? I wasn't about to just let him go without me. He's my best friend."

Easy clears his throat and pushes his chair back noisily, getting to his feet.

"Right," I murmur, considering what he's saying. "I just…I don't want to hold Bambi back from his dreams, but I'm not sure I'll be happy going back to the life I walked away from all those years ago. That version of me died in the car accident, you know?"

"Can you be happy here without him?" Easy asks.

I try to imagine watching Bambi get on the ferry and leave, imagining going back to the life I lived on the island during the years before I noticed him right in front of me. The thought of lying on the beach, picking up tourists, partying day in and day out, it all feels hopelessly hollow now.

"No," I answer. "So, basically, I'm damned if I do, damned if I don't."

"Here's a novel idea," Trick says, coming in on the tail end of the conversation and helping himself to coffee and donuts too. "You could just ask him what he wants for the future like an adult in a relationship."

"What would you know about adult relationships?" I arch an eyebrow at him.

"Fuck all," he says through a mouthful of donut. "But I'm right on this one."

I know he is. I've been avoiding the subject with Bambi because I've been afraid of the answer, terrified of making this decision together, but I think we've put it off long enough. When I get home today, I will tell him that I'm all in whether he wants to stay here, go back to New York, or move to the fucking moon.

I'm all in.

BAMBI

The second time I wake up, I'm alone in Ten's bed. I roll over to find a note resting on the cool pillow next to me.

Bambi,

Went to Easy's for a bit. I'll be back a little later. I didn't make coffee, but I did text Raven to drop some off for you, so there's a good chance it's already waiting for you in the kitchen.

Love,

Ten

I smile and read the simple note a few more times. It's a small thing, and maybe it's silly, but no one has ever been this concerned about whether or not I get my morning coffee. The *love* at the end is pretty fucking awesome too. Would it be crazy to have this note framed so I can stare at it forever?

I set it down on his nightstand and crawl out of bed, wincing at the tender ache in my ass before smiling again. I clench and hiss at the slight pain, the perfect reminder of what Ten and I shared early this morning. I wonder if I can talk him into being inside me every single day so the ache never fades.

I head straight for my bathroom to take a shower. I'm covered in dry, crusted cum and sand from the beach. A startled laugh falls from my lips when I catch a glimpse of myself in the mirror, remnants of my makeup from last night still smeared all over my face. How Ten had sex with me this morning without laughing himself silly is a mystery.

I step under the hot spray and groan. I lather up the bar of tropical-scented soap I got from Goose a few days ago and the delicious smell fills the steamy space. I gasp when I slide my sudsy hand between my ass cheek, feeling slickness leaking from my hole, a combination of lube and Ten's cum. I slip a finger inside myself, reveling in the burn again.

My cock gives a lazy twitch but doesn't fully harden. I slip my finger back out and finish washing. Once I'm dried and dressed, I wander into the kitchen to find coffee from Raven's waiting on the counter, just like Ten promised.

While I sip, I consider what I want to do today. Now that my morning sluggishness has been chased away by the coffee and the shower, I'm feeling energized and refreshed, like I woke up as a whole new person this morning.

Everything feels possible, even finding a compromise that will make both Ten and I happy without having to give up this beautiful thing we're building. I go into the living room to pet Fred and Barney, giving each of them treats. Watching a movie is an option, or maybe taking down the Halloween decorations since it's November first now, but I want to do something more active than that.

I want to surf, but I'm not going to do that alone. With my luck, I'd end up drowning. So, I decide on the second-best thing. I pull on a pair of tennis shoes and write a note to Ten to let him know I'm going for a hike to the waterfall, and that I'll be home in a few hours, just in case he gets home before I do, and then I head out.

It's already late in the morning but still a little bit cool out, with a slight breeze wrapping around me as I make my way toward the mountain. I stop when I reach the trailhead, trying to remember which one we took to finally find the waterfall. I'm pretty sure it was the far left one, but even if it's not, there's not *that* much mountain to get lost on. I can always just turn around and come back if I don't find the waterfall.

With an unearned sense of confidence, I make my way into the trees, following the unkempt trail into the woods.

While I walk, I let my mind wander, thinking about Ten, about the past and the future, about my dad and my life. The quiet of the mountain as I make my way through the thick of the trees seems to burrow inside me, bringing me a sense of peace and clarity I feel like I've been searching for my whole life. I'm still not one hundred percent sure yet what I want to do about med school, but I feel like whatever I decide will be the right thing.

Maybe that's what Raven meant, that he couldn't tell me the path because whatever I choose will be the correct one. I just need to make a decision and commit to it. Either way, I know I'm not going to give up Ten. He's the one. If there was ever a question about that, he's the answer.

The trees seem to get thicker, the path even more overgrown the farther up the mountain I go. Nothing looks familiar, but I'm not sure how much attention I was paying the first time. I'll go a little farther and turn around if it still doesn't look right.

I forge ahead, whistling into the quiet, delighted when birds match their songs to my tune.

The trees start to thin again, and I pick up my pace, sure the clearing with the waterfall will be right ahead. I'm craning my neck, trying to spot the birds in the trees overhead, not paying much attention to where my feet are landing when the ground seems to disappear beneath me.

I barely have time to gasp, my arms flailing as I careen out of control, tumbling down the steep incline I didn't see coming. There's nothing to grab on to until I painfully crash onto an outcropped ledge, wide enough to catch my body and stop me from falling any farther.

"Fuck," I gasp, the air punched out of my lungs and my head swimming.

It takes several seconds to get my bearings,

looking up at how far I've fallen. It's far enough that I will have to climb if I want to make it back up there. I get to my feet, gasping when a sharp pain shoots up my leg and it gives way beneath me.

Double fuck.

Okay, this is going to be fine. I'm not panicking, definitely not panicking.

I grope for my phone in my pocket and come up empty.

Triple fuck.

"Little help here, Harold?" I call out to no one.

Okay, so maybe I'm panicking a little.

CHAPTER 23

TEN

I'm not all that concerned when I get home to find a note from Bambi that he went for a hike. Confused and surprised, yes, but not concerned. I'm not even all that worried when he's not home by the late afternoon, figuring he probably is just enjoying the hike, maybe lingering at the waterfall longer than he expected.

When the sun begins to set and he's still not home, I start to worry. Knots form in my stomach as I pace the kitchen, considering whether it would be an overreaction to go looking for him. There's surprisingly good cell reception even up on the mountain, so he would call if there was a problem, wouldn't he?

I absently scroll through my phone, doing my best to keep calm and talk my heart into beating normally. I wander into my bedroom, and my heart plummets when my eyes land on Bambi's phone resting on the top of my dresser.

"Shit," I mutter, pulling my phone out of my pocket like a gunslinger, my heart in my throat and my hands trembling with anxiety.

"Yo," Easy answers, completely oblivious to the panicked fog I'm currently enveloped by.

"Bambi's out on the mountain, and I think he might be lost. Call everybody and bring flashlights." I don't even wait for him to respond before I hang up my phone, shove it back into my pocket, and practically sprint out of the house.

By the time I reach the base of the mountain, there's already a small crowd of locals milling around, holding flashlights or using their phones, all looking as worried as I feel.

"Do you know where he was going?" Devil asks as soon as I'm close enough.

"He said the waterfall, but fuck knows how turned around he might have gotten."

A few of them nod solemnly.

"Let's split up then," Easy suggests. "He's smart enough to stick to a trail at least, so if a few of us take each one, we should be able to find him. He's probably just having a hard time in the dark."

I'm sure he's right, but that doesn't do anything to ease the worries making my skin prickle and my heart flail. It feels like something more is wrong, but I can't put my finger on why I'm so sure.

"We'll find him," Boston agrees confidently, and I nod, trying to stay positive.

Rapid footfalls echo on the street behind me, and I turn to find Raven sprinting toward the group.

"Bambi's hurt," he says as he skids to a halt, dragging in ragged breaths.

"Fuck," I growl. "Do you know where he is?"

Raven shakes his head with an apologetic expression.

There are more groups of people joining the crowd, and I'm vaguely aware of Easy and Trick shouting instructions, maybe forming the search parties. I don't have a fucking clue, and I don't care. I need to find Bambi, and I can't stand around here and wait for everyone to get organized. I click on my flashlight and pick a random trail, barreling into the woods with a single-minded mission.

Even with my flashlight, I can hardly see two feet in front of my face. Night has descended quickly, and the trees block any light from the moon, leaving me wandering through pitch darkness, only a small circle of illumination guiding my way.

"Bambi!" I shout. "Ryan!" I just hope he's conscious. If he fell and hit his head, we might not find him until the sun comes up again. "Ryan!"

Tree branches whip at my face, but I barely register them. Nothing matters except finding Bambi. And then I'm going to kiss the fuck out of him and tell him he'd better never scare me like this again.

I'm not sure how long I follow the trail, calling out his name over and over until my voice gets hoarse. How far would he have gone before realizing he was lost and turning around? I might not even have the right trail, he could've picked a different one. I force myself to stop and pull out my phone to check for updates. Maybe someone else has found him already.

Nothing.

"Fuck!" I shout into the air, my voice echoing off the mountain and the trees, into the vast sky above.

I drag in deep breaths, trying to force my rising panic down as I consider what I should do. Do I keep going up? Turn around and pick another trail? Would Bambi have wandered off the trail altogether? Easy didn't seem to think so, but sometimes these damn trails are so overgrown it's hard to tell when you've stepped off. If he wasn't paying attention, it's possible he wandered off without even realizing it.

A sound to my left draws my attention. It sounds like whistling. My heart leaps, and I take off toward it. It's faint. I have to stop every few feet to hear it over the sound of my footsteps through the overgrown weeds, but it's the same tune that Bambi was whistling that night at the bar, what feels like a million years ago now, while we were cleaning up together.

I follow the sound as it gets louder until I find myself standing on the edge of the mountain.

"Bambi," I call out, turning around, hoping I'll see him somewhere off to one side or the other.

"Ten," a voice rasps quietly.

"Bambi." I whip back around and shine my flashlight down, bile and fear rising in my throat as I spot him several yards down the side of the mountain. "Jesus," I mutter, dropping onto my stomach and crawling near the edge to look over. "Are you all right?"

"Fucking peachy," he answers, his voice sounding raw like he's been calling for help for hours. He probably has.

"Shit. I don't have a rope or anything. Goddammit. I sure know how to put together a rescue effort, don't I?" I look around in the dark as if an answer will suddenly appear, and then I remember that I'm not up on the mountain alone.

I pull out my phone and call Easy, describing the location and telling him what we need to get Bambi out of here safely.

"I'm on it," he says quickly, and we hang up.

The next hour is a blur. Luckily, the guys had enough foresight to pack shit I was too panicked to think of, like rope and water bottles. We manage to get Bambi back up to safe ground, but his leg is too injured to walk on.

Trick helps him climb onto my back, and I finally breathe easily again once his arms and legs are wrapped around me, his weight as I carry him down the mountain more than welcome.

"How'd you find him so far off the trail?" Lux asks as we hike through the darkness, Bambi's chin resting on my shoulder.

"I heard him whistling."

"What?" Bambi says. "I wasn't whistling."

"Yeah, it was the same song from the last night we closed up the bar," I argue.

"I swear, I wasn't. I was shouting for hours, and I lost my voice, and once it got dark, I was just lying there hoping for a miracle."

"Then who the fuck was whistling?" I ask.

Easy hums *The X-Files* theme song, and we all laugh. Maybe it was the ghost of Harold Tellinson helping me find Bambi, or maybe I was so panicked I was hearing things. He's safe now, and that's really the only damn thing I care about.

BAMBI

"How does it look?" I ask, wincing as Ten gently probes my swollen ankle with his fingers while the guys buzz around us in the kitchen. Boston said he was going to get me something to eat and then disappeared, but everyone else followed us all the way back to the house like a flock of ducklings, all asking over and over if I was okay.

"I don't *think* it's broken, but we're going to have to get you to a hospital on the mainland for an x-ray. In the meantime, I can wrap it," Ten answers.

I nod, relaxing in the chair and letting him get to work on me with the help of his well-stocked first-aid kit.

"Here, have some water." Goose hands me a glass, and I guzzle it down, handing it back to him empty a second later.

"That's what this island needs," I muse, watching Ten work deftly with the ace bandage, his brow furrowed in concentration.

"What's that?"

"A doctor."

He looks up at me with a smirk. "We have a doctor." He winks.

"No, I mean like a clinic. We need someone who *wants* to be the doctor here, so we don't all have to go to the mainland for emergencies and, hell, even physicals, STI tests, all of that. We have to make a trip for *all* of that."

"Dude, it would be fucking awesome to have a clinic here for some of that," Easy says enthusiastically.

A feeling of excitement rises inside me, a sense of *rightness*. *This* is why I'm here. I don't know how I know that, but I do. I can feel it in my bones the same way I know Ten is it for me and the sky is blue. They're inarguable truths.

"That's what I'm going to do."

He finishes wrapping my ankle and looks up at me. "You're going to open a clinic here?"

"Yeah. I mean, obviously, I need to finish med school first and actually become a doctor." That's when the wind goes out of my sails, and I frown.

Ten stares at me for several seconds, our eyes meeting as we both seem to process this information. If I'm going to do this, it will mean leaving the island for a few years at least, leaving *him*. The decision doesn't even have to be made. I've already decided. This is what I'm meant to do.

I open my mouth to tell Ten that I can come visit all the time, that we'll make it work while I'm in school, that I'll do whatever it takes, but he beats me to it.

"Okay, I'll come with you."

"What?" I pull my leg out of his grasp, biting back a gasp at the pain that radiates through me. "You can't do that."

"Sure, I can. Why not?" He starts pulling items out of his first-aid kit to clean up my cuts and scrapes.

"Because you love the island. You don't want to come live in New York with me while I finish school and everything."

His eyes meet mine again, his expression more serious than I've ever seen it. "I love you more. If this is the answer the island finally gave you, then I'm in. We'll go, and then when you're finished making it official, we'll come back and open a clinic here together."

Shock ricochets through me, but as soon as he says it, I can see it. The island doesn't *need* two doctors, but why the hell not? We can work side by side, take care of everyone here, and enjoy the island for the rest of our lives. It feels exactly right. It feels perfect.

I smile at him. "Let's do it."

CHAPTER 24

TEN

"What did they say?" I ask, unable to even pretend I haven't been sitting on pins and needles while he had a call with his adviser about resuming classes.

It's been almost a month since we made the decision, and there have been a lot of back and forth emails while he did his best to prove that he's feeling emotionally fit again and ready to get back to school.

He crosses the living room toward me. I open my arms, and he straddles my lap without hesitation, carding his fingers through my short hair. His leg healed up well from the sprain he got in the fall. The healing time has kept us in the house a *lot* lately, and I'm not about to complain about all the one on one time, that's for sure.

"They said I'm cleared to come back for the spring semester of classes which starts in January."

He grimaces as he imparts the news as if

he's expecting I'm going to tell him that's too soon or I've changed my mind. No way in hell am I changing my mind. Bambi and I are officially a package deal from here on out. Where he goes, I go.

Instead of telling him this for the millionth time, I grab a handful of his T-shirt and tug him in for a kiss, claiming his lips fiercely to erase any doubt about how I feel.

"That sounds great. We can find an apartment right away and take the ferry in two weeks. That way we'll have time to settle in before you have to start classes."

He nods, his forehead bumping mine. "Okay. But do we have to do that today?"

"What did you have in mind instead?" I ask, putting my hands on his thighs and nibbling at his lips again, as addicted to the little sighs he makes and the flavor of his mouth as I've ever been.

A slow smile spreads over his lips. "An adventure."

"Okay, let's go on an adventure." I press one more full kiss to his lips before he climbs off my lap and offers me his hand.

I don't bother to ask him where we're going. I just put on my shoes and follow him out of the house. Truly, I would follow Bambi anywhere.

As he leads me through town, a mixture of sadness and anticipation weaves its way through me. Even if we're only going to be away for a few years, I will miss the island and everyone on it. There's not a single doubt in my mind that I'm making the right choice though.

Bambi glances back at me over his shoulder, the late-morning sun making his blond hair look like a halo around his head. I lunge forward to scoop him into my arms, and he squeals with laughter as I hold him to my chest and kiss his neck.

"Maybe I need to rethink this whole thing. You're clearly not domesticated for normal society."

"Of course I'm domesticated," I scoff. "Remind me, am I allowed to do nude yoga in Central Park?"

He shakes his head, and I put him down. "You're impossible, but I fucking love you."

"That's convenient because I fucking love you too."

When we reach the base of the mountain, Bambi confidently picks a trail.

"Hey, Magellan, are you sure you know where we're going?" I tease.

"First almost drowning and now this. I'm always going to be a joke to you, aren't I?" He tsks. "I know where I'm going this time."

"Okay, let's do it." I follow him into the woods, figuring at least I'm with him this time so I can catch him if he tries to walk off the side of the mountain again.

It doesn't take long before I know where he's leading me, but I still act surprised for him when we step into the meadow, the rainbow carousel gleaming in the sun, looking beautiful with her fresh coat of paint.

He presses a few buttons on the control panel, and this time it comes to life immediately.

"I guess Goose fixed something after all," I say, hopping on and offering Bambi my hand to pull him aboard as well.

"Or our love is so strong now that we can power this thing from space." There's only a slight hint of teasing in his tone.

I gasp playfully. "Are you saying you believe in the legends now?"

I steady myself with a hand around one of the poles, and he leans against me, tilting his head up to grin at me. "I believe that I love you more than I ever thought was possible. Maybe that's the only magic we need to worry about."

I dip my head and catch his lips with mine. That's plenty of magic for me.

BAMBI

I climb onto one of the horses, sliding forward as much as I can and patting its ass to invite Ten to join me. It's a tight squeeze, but we manage it. The plastic beast rises and falls slowly as the carousel moves in its dizzying circles. I lean back into Ten, tilting my head against his shoulder as he wraps his arms around me.

"Okay, so, med school and then back here to open a small clinic," I say.

"Mm-hmm," he agrees, dragging his lips teasingly along the side of my throat.

"Then what?"

"Then we live, Bambi. We help people around here by making sure their dicks don't fall off from overuse, we treat their surfing and hiking injuries, we make sure everyone is happy and healthy. And when we're not doing that, we learn every inch of this mountain by hiking it, we hit the waves until you're an expert on a surfboard, we laugh and play and love, we enjoy every fucking day we have on the most beautiful island in the world."

My heart feels unbearably full. I close my

eyes, and I can picture every single thing. Sure, we'll have to leave for a little while, but it's a small price to pay for forever.

"And when we die, we get to haunt this place too, right?" I check.

"Oh, absolutely," Ten agrees solemnly. "I wonder if Harold and George were hot. Do you think ghost orgies are a thing?"

I laugh loudly, the sound echoing into the wide-open sky. "I can't believe I didn't know how weird you were before. I spent two years swooning so hard over you, and it turns out you are the biggest goofball alive."

"You were crushing on me for two years?" he asks, sounding delighted and surprised.

"How did you not know that? I was *not* subtle. Every single time you looked at me, I blushed so hard I nearly fainted."

"I just thought you were shy. I did love that blush though." He can't seem to stop kissing me, brushing his lips here and there, on every inch of skin he can find. I never want him to stop.

"This is nice," I say with a content sigh, leaning all of my weight on him, feeling the rise and fall of his chest against my back.

"It's perfect," he agrees.

"Can we stay here all afternoon?" I ask

wistfully. "I just want to live in this bubble here with you for a little while before we have to start planning what comes next."

"We can stay here as long as you want. I told you, this island is ours."

And so, we stay, wrapped up in each other, picking out shapes in the clouds and getting lost in slow, heady kisses until the sky starts to turn a pale shade of pink. We talk about our future and our dreams, and when we leave, we tell Harold we'll be back…you know, just in case he's super invested in our happily ever after.

Then, we walk hand in hand back down the trail and into town, not in any particular rush but more than ready to face what comes next…together.

EPILOGUE

STORM

Music plays from someone's phone, barely audible over the sound of the ocean, the crackling of the massive bonfire and the sound of drunken revelry going on all around.

What the fuck am I even doing here? I hate this kind of stuff—putting on an awkward smile, grappling for small talk when we know good and well we've got nothing in common, acting like I remotely fucking belong here among all of these wild, carefree people who've made the island their home.

My phone vibrates in my pocket, and my jaw clenches reflexively. I should chuck it into the ocean, get a new phone and a new number, and call it a day. There's nothing stopping me, no one I'm *hoping* to hear from. The thought of it is freeing, but I stop myself from following through.

Maybe part of me isn't as ready to let go of the past as I like to think, or maybe I just hate the idea of change.

"They look happy, don't they?" Hennessey surprises me by appearing out of the shadows with a Solo cup extended in my direction.

I look at the cup and then at him, a slightly drunk smile tilting his lips, just the littlest bit of a sway to his body as he stands beside me, reminding me of the steady in and out of the tides. He's not wasted, but he's not far off either.

I take the cup and follow the direction of his gaze to see Ten and Bambi with eyes only for each other. If you would've told me a few months ago that *anything* would get Ten to leave the island, even for a few years, I would've said you were crazy.

Actually, I likely would've snorted and stared blandly, but same difference, honestly. The way he's looking at Bambi, though, I'm pretty sure the kid could've asked him to move to the moon together and he would've agreed.

I wonder if the whole island would come together to throw me a going-away party if I decided to leave? The thought is almost laughable. The entire lot of them would starve to death without me here, so there's that at least. If you can't be affable, be useful—I'm sure someone famous said that.

Ten leans over and kisses Bambi, the two of them getting so lost in each other I'm sure the ocean could catch fire and they wouldn't notice.

My stomach twists, and I force a smile for Hennessey's sake, grunting in acknowledgment.

"You think all of that silly, romantic Harold Tellison stuff is real?" he asks, the wistful edge to his voice undermining his attempt at mocking the island legends.

"No," I answer simply, feeling like an utter dick when his face falls.

"Right, me either."

Fuck. I awkwardly reach out toward him, not sure if putting a hand on his shoulder is the right move as far as apologizing for my callousness. Put me in my kitchen, and I know what I'm doing. I'm confident...maybe *too* confident sometimes, but one-on-one with people in the wild? Yeah, I'm a shit show.

"Anyway, sorry to bother you. Have a good night, Chef," Hennessey says, slowly backing away.

I watch him go with a sense of regret filling my chest. It's not like it's the first time I'm sure he thought I was a dickhead, given how heated I can get when I'm in the kitchen, but I'd love to leave a good impression on *someone* just once in my life. There's always next time, I suppose.

"I don't know what the hell I'm going to

do for a bartender now," Boston grumbles from a few feet away.

"You want Lyric?" Easy offers quickly. "He's always late and a few buds short of a bag if you ask me, but he's hot, which is really the most important thing in a bartender, right?"

Boston strokes his beard, seeming to consider it. "Sure, why the hell not. If he's interested in the job, I'll give him a shot."

"I'll shoot him a text in the morning," Easy says, and Boston claps him on the shoulder in thanks.

My phone vibrates in my pocket for the umpteenth time, and I finally pull it out to see what the hell is so important. As I suspected, I have a dozen texts waiting for me that I'm not the least bit interested in reading, but I click the icon anyway and scroll to the latest one.

DONNIE: Dammit, Seth. I need to talk to you. You can't spare FIVE minutes for your husband? Call me!

Ex-husband, I mentally correct before deleting the entire text thread without responding. I shove my phone back away and find my eyes wandering over to where Hennessey is, swaying in the sand to the beachy tune that's playing. Was I ever that young or carefree?

He stops dancing and looks in my direction. Our eyes meet across the fire. The light from the flames flickering over his face gives him an eerie sort of beauty that makes my heart beat a little faster before I manage to shake it off.

I think if my train wreck of a marriage to Donnie proved anything, it's that I'm better off alone. Besides, no matter how hard a person tries on an island like this, they're never *really* alone.

THE END

Printed in Great Britain
by Amazon